SOJOURN IN MOSAIC

SOJOURN IN MOSAIC

ROBERT A. ELFERS

Friendship Press • New York

This is a work of fiction. The remarks that appear in quotation marks in the book and the characters to whom they are attributed are imaginary representations. They are based on the author's observations but they are fictional. No resemblance should be construed between these characters and real people, living or dead.

Library of Congress Cataloging in Publication Data

Elfers, Robert A.
Sojourn in Mosaic

I. Title.
PZ4.E3775So [PS3555.L385] 813'.5'4 79-10244
ISBN 0-377-00089-2

For Edie

Editors' Note

Sojourn in Mosaic represents a unique endeavor in fictional work. The originating idea for a work of fiction representing some aspects of life in the Middle East came from the workings of a task force of the Commission on Education for Mission. That idea was then transformed and given life by the author, Robert A. Elfers. A fictional piece, *Sojourn in Mosaic* intends both to excite the reader to further study on the Middle East and to provide as much authentic background as is possible. It is the editors' judgment that the book does both. The character representations and the background information represent the impressions of the author and are based on the author's own thinking, experiences and conversations with persons in the Middle East. For those of you who are part of a group studying the Middle East we commend the related resources listed on the back cover of this book. But to all readers, whether part of a study group or reading for enjoyment, we invite you to enjoy and respond to this story and thus to take your own "sojourn in mosaic".

CHAPTER
ONE

THE taxi dispatcher sent me to the Salters' address. I didn't realize it was theirs until I pulled up in front of the house. The last time I'd been here was ten years or so ago, soon after I got out of the army.

The door opened immediately and a woman—their housekeeper—helped old Harry Salter and Theresa, his wife, down the steps. The woman told me where they wanted to go as they entered the cab. I nodded, keeping my face turned away, hoping they wouldn't see who I was.

Old Harry and I were distantly related, the way a lot of people are in West Virginia. When I had a chance, I took a quick look at him and Theresa in the mirror. They looked a good deal older. Well, I was a lot older, too. Those had been pretty good days, that long decade in the past. I used to see the Salters then, once in a while; it was like them to warm up to my mother and brother and me when they thought I was bettering myself. Funny how people are. You can be nothing more than poor kin from back up in the valley and then a high school coach shows you how to play football, colleges offer you scholarships, Uncle Sam lets you boss some grunts around in his army.

You're still Amon Smith, but people walk across the street to shake your hand and those thin little blood ties with folks like the Salters grow warm and thick and cozy.

Good days. They seemed so then, anyway. But in the past, all over. Everything had gone downhill since then, and I hadn't seen anything of old Harry or Theresa along the way. That was why I didn't want to see them that afternoon, and hoped they wouldn't recognize me.

But when we got hung up at the tracks, waiting for a string of empty coal cars to rumble by, old Harry leaned forward and rapped me on the shoulder. "How are you, Amon?"

He and Theresa were friendly and decent enough not to mention Nancy or the business. I felt I had to say something about the cab, so I told them I was driving it just to keep busy while I did some thinking.

We didn't go far. When they got out, Theresa reached out a hand to steady herself and bent her head to say something to me through the open window. I had to lean over to hear her weak voice.

"We've had hard times, too, you know," she said. "We know how it feels to be alone."

She meant all right, I suppose, but I wished I hadn't met them. They stirred up memories that hurt at the end of a so-so day. I drove to my empty house because there was no place else to go.

When I want to, I can put together a pretty good meal. I made an effort that night, but I wasn't really hungry. I tried watching television and then reading, but nothing worked, so I just went out and sat on the steps. I could imagine what the Salters had said after they'd seen me: "Quiet, wasn't he? Must be lonesome, with his mother gone, too, and his brother out in California. Wonder if he still lives in that house of Nancy's and his. I suppose he wouldn't go back to that old farm where he lived when he was a boy, before his daddy ran off. Can't be much there now, compared to what he and Nancy had. Of course, the two of them had problems, too, from what I've heard. Maybe that's why he's taken things so badly. But he's young. He could marry again. If he'd held on to that business. . . . But he just let it go."

That's right, I let it go. It just didn't mean anything. Some people say that I liked her father's business more than I loved her, which wasn't true. We just didn't get off the ground somehow. My fault, I guess. It takes time to be married, and we didn't have time. I was trying to get a grip on the construction trade. And I had to get away sometimes. Was it my fault that I liked hunting with good

2

buddies more than dabbling in the arts, the way she did? I didn't realize why we began to go different ways. I didn't have time to make things better. What's a year or two together? Not nearly enough time. Suddenly on a February night, she was driving home alone from a meeting of the Children's Aid Society, she hit a patch of ice on Route 19, and that was it, all done beneath the crumpled roof of her Pontiac.

Time passes. There's no use trying to forget. You just remember and remember, until you wear memory out. But then it comes back when you see someone from the past, as I had that day. Then you just hang on, sitting on your front steps on a cloudy night.

I watched the sky for a while. Once or twice, wisps and patches of white silver showed and I waited for the moon to come out. It didn't. Then my phone rang.

"This is Harry Salter."

No nonsense, no mention of our meeting that day. Just, "Can you get over tomorrow to see me? I want to talk with you about a private matter. I need some help and I'm willing to pay for it." We agreed to meet at the office he kept in the Anthracite Building, when my shift was over the next day.

I was late getting there. That afternoon, we had a windy, lashing storm that flooded the streets and threw mist against the hills and down the valleys. I had been driving steadily and I ached from wetness and fatigue. He had a little reception room but no one was there, so I rapped on his office door. He called me in.

It was dark in the room, but his desk lamp was on, etching his face in bone and shadow. With the ominous clouds racing by outside his window, he didn't look so much old as primeval. He'd been a hard man all his life and he'd made a lot of money working coal and oil and gas and pushing people out of his way.

"Like to show you something," he said. A piece of equipment like a little TV set was at one end of his big, black walnut desk. He fumbled with it until the screen lit up. There were some buildings in the background, and a stretch of lawn in front. The camera followed a figure walking across the grass: a thin, blonde young woman dressed in jeans and a light shirt with the tails out. Her hair was long; she was hugging something—a box or books—to her breast. She suddenly realized she was being photographed, smiled a little, and turned her head away. The screen went blank.

"Now listen to this," he said and raised a sheet of paper into the lamplight to read:

"You just don't understand. Your answers aren't my answers. They don't work for me. I appreciate all that you have done and

3

know that you have tried to be loving. But it's no use. I've decided to get out of your life for a while."

Harry Salter had started reading in that high, hard voice of his, strictly impersonal, but I could tell when he got a little choky and his tongue tripped over words that the stuff was getting to him.

"I'm going away," he read. "I know where I want to go and I've been saving money. Your lives will be easier, I hope, without the burden of trying to direct someone who cannot accept your direction. You have given me many things and, although I know it will seem heartless, I'm asking you to give me one thing more: the freedom to find my own way. It's not always been easy to love you, but I want you to know that I do now. I hope you will love me despite what I'm doing."

He dropped the paper on his desk and buried himself back in his leather chair, his face out of the light. After a moment, he said, "The girl in the movie is our daughter, Mary. That film is all I have to show you of her as a grown-up. I got the film from someone who knew her at college. Her mother hasn't seen it. I'm afraid to show it to her. I don't think she could stand seeing it."

"And Mary wrote the letter?"

"Yes, sir," he said, almost as if he were confessing a crime. Maybe he was. I really didn't care. I did want to know what all that had to do with me.

"What do you think of the letter?" he demanded.

"Well, I guess it's a problem a lot of families have these days." I was thinking it was a problem rich families had. My mother and brother and I hadn't had problems like that when I was growing up. We stuck together to get by, raising beans and things on the hillside and trapping rabbits in the woods to add to what we got from relief.

"You should remember her, Amon. We had an open house for some of you men just back from Vietnam. She was serving punch."

I said maybe I did. I had a dim recollection of a thin little thing, too shy to look at you for longer than a peep. I might have remembered her more clearly, but Nancy was at that open house, too, the first time I saw her, and everything else was out of focus.

Harry Salter was saying something and I realized that he had asked me a question. "Excuse me?"

"I said I'll pay you $100 a day plus expenses. If you find her, there will be a generous bonus." He leaned forward into the light again and stretched out his bony hand to me. "Agreed?"

To this day, I don't know why I did it. Those storm clouds rolling behind the rain-and-wind-streaked windows, that piece of paper lying in the circle of lamplight, those old, weary eyes and that wrinkled hand reaching at me—I didn't know what they were demanding of me. Maybe that was it. I was tired of what I knew. It was what I didn't know that I wanted.

"Agreed," I said, and shook his hand. I didn't even know where he thought Mary was, or why.

*   *   *

Istanbul?

"That's a long way to go," I told him. I was surprised. I'd thought she might be in San Francisco or Toronto or some place like that.

"Never mind how far it is. Go wherever is necessary. Just find her and tell her that her mother and I want to see her. We'd like to have her home a while. We feel she owes us that."

"What makes you think she'll come? That letter sounds like she's pretty independent."

"I don't know that she will. But I want you to tell her what I said. The reason I picked you, Amon, is that you're family. Distantly related, but still family. This is family business."

I thought for a minute. "That means it's confidential and you'd prefer that I didn't go to police or U.S. embassies?"

"That's right. But I think you can do it. There's someone right in Clarksburg who can help. Do you know somebody named Anita Merkosian? She's Armenian."

I didn't, but the next day took care of that shortcoming. Harry had told me she ran Big M Truckers, a company that he did business with, but that was my only preparation for the interview. When I parked among the hulking semis at the trucking terminal and was ushered into her office, I looked at her and said, "You're Mrs. Merkosian?"

My incredulity showed through and she snapped back at me in a loud, husky voice, "Yes, I am. What does Harry Salter want you to get out of me?"

She was a short, heavy old woman, dressed in black, her iron grey hair pulled into a little bundle at the back of her head. Her face was wrinkled and dark, and her eyes glinted at me like hard coal. I knew right away I'd made her mad.

"Excuse me if I sounded surprised, ma'am. I knew about you but I just didn't expect . . . . "

"Never mind," she interrupted testily. "I told Harry I'd seen his

5

daughter in Istanbul. That was two years ago, and when I mentioned it to him when I got back here, he hardly seemed interested. Now he sends you over to ask me about her. Well, I'll tell you what I told him. I saw her at a trucking center. She had some foolish notion about hitching a ride south to one of the Arab countries."

"I get the idea from her father that she's a freaky rich kid," I said, hoping to ingratiate myself by revealing a bias against the younger generation. But Mrs. Merkosian was flinty, and I hurriedly tried another tack.

"It interests me to know," I said, "that you were in Turkey when you saw her. I knew an Armenian guy in the army. He told me he and his people didn't want anything to do with Turks."

"You don't know me, young man, and you don't know Mary Salter. And your attitude toward the Armenian people is ignorant as well."

"Please, Mrs. Merkosian . . . . "

"Are you aware that Armenia was the first nation in the world where Christianity became the national religion? That was back in the fourth century. Do you realize that Armenians were part of the Roman legions in Jerusalem during Roman occupation? Do you know that many of those Armenian Legionnaires became Christians and were martyred for their faith? Do you know that part of the Old City of Jerusalem is known as the Armenian quarter because Armenians have been in Jerusalem, helping to keep Christianity alive there, for so long?"

"No, not really," I confessed.

"And what do you know about the Turks, other than that they persecuted the Armenians in the first part of the Twentieth Century?"

I waited for her to continue, and she seemed to calm down a little.

"Istanbul is a beautiful city, but unless you're rich, you put up with things that are frustrating—run-down housing and streets and sewer system. Your kids' schools aren't what they should be and there aren't enough parks for them to play in."

"About all I know about Turkey is that it's supposed to have a good army and to be against the Communists."

"You see. A typical American point of view. You look at Turkey—and all the rest of the countries in the Middle East—and you ask, Are they non-Communist, do they have oil, are they on our side?" She was getting excited again, but there was no way to stop her. "Those people over there are human beings. There are forty million of them in Turkey alone. Some of them are Armenian, my

6

family included. Only a few; 99 percent of Turks are Muslim, so you see the number of other religions—people like us Armenian Orthodox—is very small. That's hard sometimes, being such a tiny minority. The Muslims are taught to be tolerant of Christians—they revere Jesus as a prophet—but there are different kinds of tolerance. Things aren't easy over there." She raised her hands and her eyebrows in synchronized emphasis. "Seventy percent of the Turks are peasants, simple people who want nothing more than a happy family and a decent life. They love the old traditions, yet they're being pulled in new directions by being such close neighbors to Europe. Do you know thousands of Turkish men go to countries in Western Europe every year to work? They come back to their home villages changed people. Some of them even bring European wives! Can you imagine the impact they have? Most of the old folks haven't accustomed themselves yet to the changes that Ataturk brought to Turkey." She looked at me sharply. "Do you know who Ataturk was?"

Thank Gertrude Calisher! She had taught me 11th grade European history and had been a nut on great reformers, among them Kemal Ataturk, "the father of modern Turkey."

"Oh, yes," I said. "A remarkable man. If I recall, one of the things he did was to make the Turks use their own language rather than Arabic in the Muslim call to prayer."

She nodded. "That's one of many. Of course, Turks being as conservative as they are, you still hear the muezzin in Arabic in some places. How did you remember that? Are you interested in religion? Is that why Harry Salter picked you to look for Mary?"

"Not particularly. Why?"

She didn't acknowledge the question and, since she seemed a little friendlier, I didn't push it. I waited and finally she said, "My husband and I were in Istanbul, visiting family. We heard about the big trucking center there and went to see it. A lot of hauling takes place between Europe and the Arab countries, and most of it funnels through Istanbul. That's just one more way in which the Turks are coming in contact with the modern world. I saw a blonde with one of those big red packs on her back. It was Mary and she was going to thumb a ride."

"Where?"

But she ignored my question again. "Anthony—my husband—thought perhaps we might start a business over there. But right after we came home, he died. Heart. He worked too hard. This company is what he made. Big M. Big Merkosian. He was proud of it. So I run it now. My daughters are married and my son is a doctor and they all say I'm crazy." She looked at me. "Just like you thought I was crazy when you walked in and saw little old Mrs. Merkosian sitting at this big desk. What else do I have to do, what better way do I have to spend my time?"

She got to me, as so many other people got to me in the days that followed. Tiny, black-eyed, wrinkled woman—so fierce and so alone.

She must have felt something, too, for she gave me a little nod and said, "You don't tell me why you took this job for Harry Salter. Why fly a long way—ten hours maybe—to look for somebody you don't know in a part of the world that's strange? You eat that food, maybe you'll get sick. Stay in the U.S.A. and go to Florida. If you've got no money, I'll give you a job."

I laughed and shrugged. "Like you said," I answered, "what else do I have to do, what better way do I have to spend my time?"

She told me that couldn't be so, I was a young man, the world was mine. So, to make sense, and because we were becoming friends, I told her about my wife and how now, as far as living was concerned, I was just treading water.

"So you are lonely," she said.

"I suppose I am."

She got up from her chair, came over, took my arm, and led me to the door. "I think, Amon Smith, that Mary is lonely, too. I could tell you more about her, but I promised to say no more than I have told her father. There are things about her that she still needs to discover, and no one must prevent her from that. But if I were looking for her, if I wanted to help her as a friend, I would not go to Istanbul. Remember, she was leaving there."

"Where is she, then?"

Her grip on my arm tightened and she gave it a shake. "I said I can't tell. But I can give you some advice. I would learn to speak Arabic."

"Mrs. Merkosian! I don't have time," I protested. "How can I do that?"

"The best place I can think of," she persisted, "is the American University in Cairo. Why don't you pay them a visit? Who knows what you could learn?"

When I got home that night, my phone was ringing. It was Harry Salter, impatient to find out about my talk with Mrs. Merkosian. He swore when I told him that the only clue she'd given me was to go to Cairo. "That old woman never mentioned Cairo before," he sputtered. "I don't trust her." He paused. "She say anything about

Jerusalem?"

"Not a thing."

"Don't hide information from me now."

I tried to reassure him, but he hung up on me. I came close to calling him back and telling him to shove his job.

The next day he was back on the phone, no apology, but telling me that I'd better be prepared to get around to different countries over there, Mary might not be in Cairo, either.

Arranging the trip was a nuisance. After a couple of false starts, the travel agent finally told me that the easiest way to visit both the Arab countries and Israel was to fly to Amman, the capital of Jordan. I could reach the other Arab countries from there, and I could also get into Israel by going overland, crossing the Jordan River at the Allenby Bridge.

Obtaining a passport and visas took a lot of time, too, and I think Harry Salter came near to calling quits to the whole affair, he was so impatient. He damned Jews and Arabs alike. Since I was reading everything I could about them, I saw that he—and a lot of other people I knew—had very little understanding of what was going on over there.

Feeling as I did about the job, I decided that I'd give him fair exchange for his money in finding his runaway kid but that I was going to enjoy the trip whenever I had a chance. In that frame of mind, one day I walked into a camera store run by someone I'd gone to high school with, George Habib. George wasn't there but his younger brother, Steve, waited on me. I told him I was looking for a 35 mm camera to replace one that I'd lost—I'd actually given it away by mistake when I was getting rid of Nancy's things. As usual, I wanted more than I could pay for. He finally showed me a used Pentax that looked in pretty good shape, but I told him I was worried that it might break down during my trip. Not likely, he said, and anyway it was standard equipment that could be repaired almost anywhere. I still acted doubtful and he asked where I was going. I told him and he grinned all over.

"Hey, that's great!" he cried. "You know we're Lebanese? Our uncle runs a camera store in Beirut. If anything happens, tell him you're our friend. And Ali, his son, my cousin, is a medical student in Cairo. He's a camera nut and can do anything with them. Besides, you ought to get in touch with him. He can show you around when you're there."

He was so genuinely enthusiastic about it that I weakened and paid his price. After he gave me the sales slip, he wrote down his uncle's and his cousin's addresses. I stuffed them in my wallet and we shook hands. Then a thought came to me: he must be five or six years younger than me. In an off-hand way, I asked if he knew a relative of mine, a girl named Mary Salter.

"Sure. I didn't know you were related," he answered. "How is she, anyway?"

"I haven't seen her for a long time. I thought maybe you had."

He seemed surprised. "No. Not for years. She just disappeared when her father pulled her out of high school." Then, realizing he might sound critical of the family, he added, "Mary was a nice person."

I went fishing for information. "Harry Salter is a hard man," I said. "We don't always see eye to eye."

Steve took the bait. "She was very serious, idealistic. We respected her. She was just friends with this guy. I don't know, maybe she really liked him, but I think part of it was because he was a foreigner and older than she. He was an Israeli and had lived in a kibbutz and all that. A romantic figure, you know, somebody who was helping set up a new home for oppressed people. He was over here visiting one of the teachers. He went back eventually, but by then, Mary was gone. All that we ever heard was that her father was so sore about their going together that he sent her to some far-away private school to break it up. Where did she go, anyway?"

I shook my head soberly and told the truth as I waved farewell. "Harry just doesn't talk about it."

No wonder Harry had asked me if Mrs. Merkosian had mentioned Jerusalem. He probably suspected that Mary might be shacked up there with her boy friend. And I was supposed to go snooping after her and break up the romance.

Israel was on my itinerary, but I told myself I wasn't going to be a keyhole-peeper. By that time, I wasn't all that keen on going at all and I would have quit if I hadn't made the deal with Harry.

The day I left, I hired a cab to the airport. The feeder line plane took me to Pittsburgh and a couple of hours later I was at Kennedy in New York. The people at the check-in counter were Middle-Easterners, well-dressed, speaking Arabic, family groups and friends excited about our departure. I felt out of it, a stranger already.

The 747 took off pretty much on time and at midnight we dined on shishkabob and rice flavored with raisins and pine nuts. Afterwards, a movie began up ahead, but I took off my shoes and eased the seat back and went to sleep. . . .

*   *   *

We hurtle eastward through the dark. Dawn rushes to meet us and we ride smooth sunlight thereafter. Stewards—men, not women —serve breakfast on this Royal Jordanian jet; evidence that Arab tradition still tends to keep most women to their roles as wives and mothers? I walk around the plane every hour or so. Finally, staring out a window, I see cultivated fields, strip of brown beach, then water. The English Channel?

I read again a travel folder: Egypt, with a population of nearly forty million, is the largest of the Arab countries. It is half again as big as Texas in land area, but 95 per cent of the Egyptian people live on less than four per cent of the land along the Nile. Cairo is its largest city, with more than nine million people. . . .

Kids are chattering in the aisles. Adults cluster in twos and threes, talking. One short, dark-bearded man wears a clergyman's collar and a cross in the lapel of his black jacket. I wonder where he and his wife are going. Perhaps they are—I refer to the literature on Egypt to find the name again—Copts. It says that Copts are the native Christians of Egypt and direct descendants of ancient Egyptians. They believe their church was founded by St. Mark in the year 42 A.D.

The man ahead of me stands, looking back through my window. I look, too, and see a bleached, brown land, with patches of green forest. "What's that?" I ask. He is puzzled but he grins at me. I point and say "What?" again. He understands, says something in Arabic, and then carefully enunciates: "Turkey . . . ."

The land becomes craggy, fissured. The sun pours clear, pale gold heat on it. I try to absorb its strangeness. After a while, I close my eyes and doze. When I look again, we are over water. Then land again, brown sand, sweeping in undulating vastness toward the brightness of the horizon. The PA system clicks and I look at my watch as the announcement is made first in Arabic, then in English. We are arriving in Amman, Jordan; ten hours have passed. I am in the Middle East . .

The airport at Amman is surrounded by hills sandpapered to soft contours by the wind. Goats graze near the airport fence. We touch down and my fellow passengers break into applause. They're glad to be down, glad to be home. Their spontaneous pleasure is engaging and I wish I'd been friendlier with them. They crowd the aisles, eager to leave, and the PA system serenades them with American dance music.

11

I make an effort to be amused at the contrasts that are gradually enveloping me. But some impressions jar me. On the way to the arrivals area, I look back in awe at the huge jet that has ripped me out of my own time and place and brought me here. I see men in uniform, automatic rifles slung across their backs. Soldiers. I haven't seen men under arms since Vietnam. . . .

The connecting flight to Cairo is late and its passengers wait as the afternoon becomes evening. The flies buzz around us and the departures room, lacking air conditioning, has open windows that do not protect us from the screams of the jet engines on the apron outside the glass partitions. We are warm, and I notice for the first time that people are carrying jugs of water. . . .

Under way again. Smaller jet. Quick cold lunch of turkey and salad. Nightfall darkens the earth and I wish now I'd taken the travel agent's advice and asked him to get me a hotel reservation in Cairo. I wanted to pick out my own place after I got there. It's going to be a nuisance, getting there late and not having a room ready. . . .

After a while, the engines change pitch and those throat-rasping syllables crackle over the speaker again. Below us, necklaces of smoky, yellow-red lights lie criss-cross on the black velvet of the land. Then I make out the beams of auto traffic and illuminated signs, all reflecting on a carpeting of buildings carved in cubes and arches. That seductive city, Cairo, wrinkled with age, awaits below us.

We land. Applause again. Buses—new, glass boxes rolling on shiny discs—carry us to the arrivals building. The air is warm and moist and smells of soft coal or diesel fuel. We are surrounded by the trappings of a big, anonymous airport anywhere: bulky, rectangular, stone terminal glowing with lights amid a periphery of tethered jets and bug-like, darting utility vehicles.

Within, however, we are entombed in Egypt: announcements squawking in Arabic or British-accented English, travel-worn people hurrying through the great rooms, doorways guarded by expressionless soldiers dressed in battle uniform, wearing steel helmets, and gripping rifles whose barrels are tipped with short, naked bayonets. Passports are checked by officials in white uniforms with shoulder boards. I go to get my luggage and try not to stare at a group of people camped in a corner. They are turbaned and gowned men, poor people, sprawled exhausted as if dumped from ancient fields of the Nile Delta into the Twentieth Century.

The contrasts and contradictions begin to pummel me. I pick up my baggage from a conveyor belt that it shares with big, glistening, new electric fans and bedding rolls wrapped in camel-hair carpets. I obtain Egyptian currency; limp and bedraggled, the bills are too big for my wallet. A young man introduces himself, a travel agent who says he has an uncle in California. He is eager to find me hotel accommodation, but his phone calls can't get through. Reluctantly, he surrenders me to a taxi driver who seems to know the names of some hotels. His Mercedes swoops along a dark, palm-lined boulevard. We flit under lighted street signs advertising European office equipment and American soft drinks. Suddenly we plunge into Rameses Street, down a channel of shadows and colored lights, sidewalks overflowing their occupants into the street, autos with falsetto horns, antique, overloaded trucks and buses belching black exhaust, toy donkeys tapping delicately along despite the gowned figures astride their rumps.

The driver stops at a hotel, a glittering commercial palace, but when I try to pay him, he refuses, and I finally understand that he thinks I should wait until I learn if I can get in. How wise he is: There are no rooms available. Have I tried the Diplomat? The desk man at the Diplomat shakes his head sorrowfully and thinks perhaps the Royale can accommodate me.

We go from hotel to hotel. My head aches with shrieking horns and squealing brakes, my eyes burn from fumes and fatigue, my body is sore all over. The driver is defeated and, I suspect, would like to be rid of me as much as I would like to be rid of him. We stop on the rim of a bleak construction site and he shrugs his shoulders and points to his wrist watch. Forty-five minutes after midnight. How right my travel agent had been. I think of Clarksburg, W. Va., and my friends there. How good it would be . . . .

Camera store! Cousin in Cairo!

I paw into my wallet and find the sales slip. There it is: Ali Habib, Church House, Peter and Paul Street, El Zamalek, Cairo!

We take off. Down Rameses Street again. We traverse a bridge across the Nile and careen down a ramp to the right. "Zamalek," the driver announces wearily, and peers into narrow streets shadowed with palm fronds. We cruise slowly, stopping to ask directions of men chatting on dark street corners. Arabic crackles back and forth, we proceed, stop again, more directions, stop again. We are lost. We happen into a lighted intersection and find a police station, an armed constable at each corner of its little square. Brusque, friendly advice. Off again. Ah, Peter and Paul Street! That must be the place!

Everything is dark. Wall directory says "Church House Residence—Three." Driver's cigarette lighter illumines the way. Third floor. Solid oak door. Ring bell. Wait. Ring. Ring. Ring.

A noise from up the stairwell, a quavering voice. Over the railing, looking down at us as the lights go on, two women in nightgowns, old and young. I explain and they respond (in English!): "Oh, Ali's cousin? From America? Oh, he's not here. But you can stay overnight in his room if you like. It's so late, I don't know where else you could go."

Oh, lady, there isn't any place else.

CHAPTER
TWO

A T around 4 o'clock in the morning, when I was sleeping, Cairo spoke its final word of welcome. The city had been annoying my slumber, harassing me with car horns and barking dogs. But now it vaulted through the windows, funnelled into my ears, and went wailing through the chambers of my brain.

I had read about the Muslim call to prayer, but now I was hearing it for the first time—in lonely darkness. It vibrated out of an amplifier that someone seemed to have turned up full volume and placed just outside my room. Too tired to get up, I waited, subservient, until it ended. Nighttime is dispiriting to me, but never before had I felt so close to despair, so much alone, so afraid of all the darkness of human existence as I did in the moments of silence that closed in upon me.

I didn't get up until early afternoon. Exploring the hallway, I came to a stairway, heard indistinct words, and ventured down. As I reached the landing, a woman—apparently an Egyptian servant—appeared, smiled, and seemed to want to lead me somewhere. I followed her into a large room filled with dark furniture. At a long table, a man was eating lunch. He looked up at me, grinned readily, and rose with outstretched hand.

"Oh, how do you do?" he said. "I'm so glad to have company. My name is Kazuo Nakamura."

I'd had Japanese businessmen as fares in Clarksburg, so I wasn't surprised to meet one in Cairo. He seemed a gently affable person and asked me politely about my trip and my first impressions of Cairo. I told him that I was still trying to decide how I felt about the city and described being awakened by the muezzin. His face lit up.

"Isn't that wonderful!" he exclaimed. "Do you know what he was saying? He was calling, 'Come to prayer, come to salvation—for prayer is better than sleep. Rise and pray!' Think of it, all across Cairo people hear that summons at dawn. Every morning, all around the world, it rouses Muslims to prayer. Do you know how many people that means? Five hundred and thirty-eight million!"

"Well, I'd never heard it before, particularly so loud."

"The reason for that," he said, "is that there's a little room for prayer in a building just down the street. In Cairo, if you own a building and have a place for prayer set aside in it, you get a tax benefit. There's one close by, and it has a PA system. The street's narrow and the sound was piped right into your windows."

"It was strange."

Mr. Nakamura nodded. "Yes, but very important. If you want to understand Egypt or any other of the Arab countries, you must understand how important religion is. Many Muslims do not adhere to every fine point of Islam—just like Christians in the U.S.—but religion is a more important part of life in the Middle East than it is in America. Islam has great influence here. The average person's philosophy of life is religious."

"Last night, looking for a hotel, I saw places that looked like mosques," I told him. "I really don't know much about the religion. A few years ago, you saw quite a bit on TV about Black Muslims."

"Oh, there are many sects, just as there are sects in Christianity. In fact—and this is something you may be surprised to know—Islam and Christianity share some common beliefs. Christian and Muslim believe in one God; they believe his will is revealed in written scripture; they expect a final day of judgment; they believe in personal immortality. And do you know that Muslims respect the divine calling of Jesus and the message of some Old Testament prophets?"

Nakamura hesitated a moment, as if he were waiting for me to

16

react. Before I could—he was the quickest kind of man—his mood changed. "One could say," he continued soberly, "that Christianity, Islam, and Judaism have much in common, much that the world needs. What a terrible tragedy it is, what an affront to God, that Christians, Jews and Muslims sometimes do not live at peace with one another. And no place is that more true than here in this section of the world."

He seemed so depressed by the observation that I would have liked to console him, but I had to be honest. "It's the same way at home, more or less. That's one of the reasons people quit going to church."

He got up from the table, and went over to one of the large windows that opened on a small balcony. His back was to me and he was silent, so I just sat there, drinking my iced tea. After two or three minutes, he said, "Can you come over here a moment?"

We moved out on the balcony and squinted into the bright, dusty heat. "Do you see that minaret?" he asked. A slender tower, topped by a roofed platform, stood three or four hundred yards away, rising gracefully among trees and other buildings. I nodded. "And that man working down there?" Just below us, across the street, was a large excavation, its rubble-strewn devastation deserted but for one man. He was toiling in the dry, stony earth, picking up bricks, one by one, and tossing them into the bed of a battered dump truck.

"Whatever we do or do not understand, we have to stand here in awe, don't we?" he said. "That minaret, so beautiful, so expressive of man's reaching for God, speaks for all the greatness of Islam. How Mohammed inspired his followers! What a civilization came to life in the Arab peninsula! At its height, it was an empire stretching from the borders of Russia all along the southern shores of the Mediterranean and up across Spain to France. Its wisdom led the world in philosophy, medicine, mathematics, astronomy, geography, architecture. Do you know that El Azhar, founded here in Cairo in 972, is world famous as a mosque and center of Islamic studies? It may be the oldest university in the world.

"And look at that man," he said. "What keeps him there, working endlessly, at so hopeless a task? He is just one of millions, living and dead. What is the secret of their power of survival across the centuries? Why, I think it must be their faith. Islam teaches each follower that he is in the presence of God. It gives him a simple creed, 'There is no God but God, and Mohammed is the apostle of God.' It requires that he worship every day and that he fast during the month of Ramadan. He must pay alms for the support of the poor and he

17

should make the pilgrimage to Mecca. There is very clear moral guidance in the Qur'an for almost every problem of his life. Do you know that when a Muslim hears or reads the Qur'an, he feels that God himself is speaking to him?"

I caught something of his interest in the minaret and the laborer but part of it slipped by me because of Mr. Nakamura himself. He was talkative, he was emotional, and he seemed a little eccentric about religion. None of these traits matched my stereotype of the Japanese.

We went inside and he looked at his watch, explaining that he had an appointment elsewhere. I told him I needed to see someone about my accommodations. He said Angela Baker, the woman in charge, was out for the afternoon; would I like to walk with him to his appointment and let him point out some of the city's sights?

When we went out into Peter and Paul Street a few minutes later, the truck we had seen at the excavation site bumped past us, wheezing at the effort. The worker was in the driver's seat, looking down on us. Mr. Nakamura immediately waved at him and called, "Hello!" The man gave him a broad grin and a British military salute as he passed.

"Wonderfully friendly and gentle people, the Egyptians," my companion said. "You know, Cairo is one of the safest cities in the world. Be careful of the traffic, however, and if you manage to squeeze on a bus, watch your wallet."

Five minutes later, we were crossing a bridge—the 26th of July Bridge—over the Nile.

"Its name commemorates the day about twenty-five years ago when the Egyptians got rid of King Farouk," Nakamura said. "A republic was set up and eventually Nasser took charge. I don't know why they don't call it the Nasser Bridge. He was a great hero, did you know that? The American government didn't like him, but he was a visionary, a leader of all the Arab peoples. They hadn't had such an epic figure for centuries."

"Why was he so important?"

Mr. Nakamura laughed and clapped me on the shoulder. "Oh, Mr. Smith, you press me too hard. You should ask an Egyptian. Or some other Arab. They can tell you much better than a visiting preacher from the United States."

I stopped, and was almost run over by half-a-dozen sheep that a boy was shepherding along the bridge's walkway. "You're a minister? From the States?"

He told me he was retired from interdenominational work and had been doing research in the Middle East for a book. His wife had

18

been with him, but had gone home early to help their daughter-in-law in Atlanta with their newly-born grandson.

I usually feel fairly easy with the clergy, thanks to a mother-enforced church-going boyhood, but Nakamura was obviously something different. I tried to figure him out as we walked along. It wasn't easy, for he was intent on helping me learn about Cairo and maintained a running commentary on customs, landmarks, costumes, economy and politics.

On the other side of the bridge, we turned down the Corniche-el-Nil, a broad, tree-lined avenue bordering the river. Before I could ask any more questions, he inquired, "Well, now, what about you, Mr. Smith? Tell me where you're from and why you're here."

I hedged for a moment, trying to answer with an affable generality that said nothing. But when Mr. Nakamura gave me a quick look of incomprehension and innocent interest, I knew he'd see I was covering up. So I told him as we walked along. Surprisingly, I felt good about it.

"How interesting," he said. "You're on an errand of mercy then. I'm not surprised. You seem to be that kind of person."

I shrugged. "I'm not sure Mary Salter will agree with you. If I find her."

"Oh, I think you'll find her," Mr. Nakamura told me. "I have that feeling about you. You get what you go after."

His confidence in me was flattering, and I felt compelled to remark that I hadn't made an outstanding success of everything I had tried. He was a good listener, and before I knew it, I told him a good deal about myself and Nancy and the rest of it.

When I mentioned that I was at the Church House by accident and wasn't sure that I could stay there, he wrote me a note to give to Angela Baker, asking her to put me up.

"I'd tell her myself," he said, "but I'll be away for a few days. I wrote her to let you have my room, if she's cramped." He pointed through the trees and the stream of traffic. "That's where I'm going, the office of one of the church groups in Egypt. They've got my luggage. I'm taking a train to a place called Minia to talk with some lay people about work they're doing."

We shook hands and I thanked him. "Maybe next time I see you, you'll have Mary Salter with you," he said cheerfully.

"I don't know," I said. "Now that I'm here, I realize what a job I've tackled. It seems like a hopeless task."

"Oh, come now," he exclaimed immediately. "Let's not speak of hopelessness. Speak of hope. Live a life of hope, Mr. Smith. Hope's the greatest thing in the world!"

I looked at him doubtfully and he put out a finger and punched me in the chest with it. He looked up at me and his eyes were alight with fire and delight. "I mean it," he declared. "Let an old preacher tell you, Mr. Smith. That's what I preach, hope. Have some. It's free."

He reached down and shook my hand again. Then, with a nod, he hurried through the deep shadows of the trees and across the pavement into a nondescript building.

I walked along a little further and opened the tourist map he had borrowed at Church House and then turned over to me. Locating where I was caused me no problem; what I didn't know was where I wanted to go. Finally, I settled on the Hilton as a temporary oasis where I could plan strategy in an air-conditioned environment.

Ten minutes later I was there and twenty minutes later I had decided it was a mistake. The public rooms were transplanted components of chrome-and-glass America. I saw a couple of blonde women in the lobby, wondered if one of them might be Mary Salter, and then ridiculed the idea. Only the faintest image of her existed in my mind, but I knew I wouldn't find her there.

So I walked back up the Corniche-el-Nil, shooing away children who came up to pose whenever I tried to photograph a boat or a group of sheep being washed at the water's edge.

Jet lag was bothering me, I guess. My thoughts wandered dispiritedly: How can I ask people about Mary Salter if I can't speak Arabic? What am I going to do if Miss What's-her-name won't let me stay longer at Church House? Why did Nakamura try to lay that stuff about hope on me?

Halfway across the 26th of July Bridge, I saw a large boat lowering its great triangular sail to pass beneath the span. I snapped a quick picture of it from one side of the bridge, dodged through the traffic to the other side, and caught it once more just as two men in the prow began to windlass the rigging up again.

As I lowered my camera, I looked up into the eyes of someone I hadn't noticed before. He was a soldier, a guard on the bridge, and he was making a bee-line for me. His face was expressionless, as impersonal as his steel helmet and his automatic rifle. Parade-ground strides brought him up to me and he grabbed my camera as if he was going to wring it from my neck. He blasted at me in Arabic. I protested in English, pointing at the boat. A crowd closed around us. The soldier kept his grip and I had a sudden vision of newspaper headlines at home: "Egypt Jails Local Man For Spying."

I appealed to the onlookers, "English? Speak English?" but their expressions—needlessly expectant, I thought—didn't change.

Then, from behind me, a woman's voice said: "Yes. What's the matter?"

I twisted around until I saw her dark glasses and curly black hair. "I don't know! I took a picture of that boat and this guy came up and grabbed me!"

She addressed him in Arabic and nodded when he rapped out a response. "You must not take pictures of the bridge," she told me. "It's forbidden. You see, it could be a military target."

"Okay, okay. Never again. I promise."

She told him what I said and he let go of the camera. The people around us smiled and I took the thing off my neck and put it into its case. I looked at the guard, but he seemed as ominously automated as ever.

"Why don't we leave?" the young woman said, and I followed her without a word.

I stole a glance at her after a few strides. She was dressed in a white blouse and a blue skirt, and wore sandals. Her skin was tanned or dark, and she had a profile that could have been Middle Eastern or European.

"Thank you," I said, loudly and slowly, wanting to be sure she understood.

"It's okay," she answered, not turning her head. I realized she must speak English as well as I and, looking at her again, I saw something familiar about her.

"Do I know you?" I asked her uncertainly.

She didn't seem to hear me and I was about to ask again when she said, "I live where you're staying. At Church House. I saw you arrive last night."

Then I recognized her; she was one of the women who had let me in. "That's twice you've helped me out," I said warmly. "I really appreciate it."

"You're welcome."

I told her about meeting and talking with Nakamura, but she didn't appear to be interested. In fact, she was rather distant. It put me off a bit and I wondered if I was being too familiar by Egyptian standards. To be proper and more formal, I told her my name and politely asked hers.

"I'm Miriam Assad," she answered. She glanced at me swiftly. "Do you plan to stay long at Church House?"

I told her I wasn't sure, and asked her what kind of place it was.

As I should have expected, she told me it was operated by English church people for religious types—students and itinerant clergy passing through Cairo.

"I hope I'm not a rotten apple in the barrel," I said. "What about you? I mean, why are you staying there? Are you a student?"

"Right now, I'm helping out with a project run by the Coptic Orthodox Church," she said, "working with garbage collectors."

"What?"

She told me that some people in Cairo made a living by collecting and using garbage. Men and teen-age boys go from door to door, picking up the stuff in mule carts. They haul it home and their families sort it out and sell it or use it some other way. Living this way isolates the garbage families from the rest of the people. They have five communities in and around the city, off by themselves because no one else will have anything to do with them. When a church worker comes to visit, he or she takes a road over garbage to families living in huts made out of stuff like old tin plates, surrounded by piles of different kinds of trash—paper, glass or tin, for example.

"What a lousy way to live," I commented. "I realize a lot of people here are poor, but if they're that poor, Cairo's in trouble. I never . . . ."

She interrupted me. "Don't misunderstand. Cairo is also rich and cultured, a great city. Egypt is a very important nation. And there are poor people everywhere—even in America. In some ways, the garbage collectors are wealthy compared to other people here. They sell what they collect, they raise pigs and cattle and sell them . . . ."

I broke in. "Pigs? I thought Muslims would have nothing to do with pigs."

"Many of the garbage collectors are Christians—maybe thirty thousand of them," she explained. "They're glad to have someone come from the church and lead services. Everyone else neglects them. They live on government land and they're forced to move every once in a while. We're trying to get that policy changed. We're helping them improve sanitary facilities. There are many ways of bringing the Gospel to them. We're encouraging them to establish one central place to sort garbage rather than each family doing it right in its own yard. We're working with them on recycling processes so they can make paper. We are establishing clinics, churches, schools—all things to help their self-respect, improve their lives, give them hope."

I wanted to ask her more, but she hadn't entirely lost her reserve, and I didn't want to offend her. We got back to Church House before I could think of any other way to keep the conversation going.

* * *

22

I met the other members of the household at the evening meal.

Angela Baker was a handsome, graying, sturdy woman from a Canadian island in the Bay of Fundy. She had been in Egypt for twenty-five years, doing different kinds of church administration jobs, now including management of Church House. In all that time, she'd been home only four or five times. I saw her almost as a figure from the past, a representative of the colonialism—the British Empire, France, the Ottoman Turks, the Romans—which had ruled Egypt in the past, but that view was corrected by another quality she had: there was something about her that spoke of friendliness for the Egyptian people, of appreciation for their attempt to build their own new nation, that illuminated and warmed her character.

A young married couple—he was from Denmark and she from Finland—were staying overnight. They left early to keep an appointment, so I learned only that he was a minister who had been a vacation replacement for the pastor of a church in Alexandria. They encouraged me to visit El Azhar and Khan-el-Kahlili, the ancient marketplace of Cairo.

There was a tall, thin man named John, from Sweden, an electronics technician who had quit that occupation to help run a mission-sponsored bookstore in Oman. He was a gregarious man who had learned American-style English during a year in the U.S. as an exchange student. He'd even been through West Virginia, and we bantered about hillbillies there and in Sweden. The most interesting thing about him was that he was studying Arabic at the American University. I didn't raise an eyebrow when he told me—but I tagged him for future questioning about Mary Salter.

Next in line—I'm remembering them as they sat at the table that night—was Miriam. She took little part in the conversation. I told the group how she had helped me that afternoon on the bridge, and she smiled at my attempts at humor but she didn't join in.

The person who surprised me the most—in a couple of ways—was Ali Habib. He arrived just as we started the soup. He was unexpected, but Angela made immediate and easy adjustments in the table and the meal continued. Both she and he sympathized with my embarrassment at intruding on his room under innocently false pretenses; their generosity and understanding made me realize that I had happened into unusual company.

Ali was different from the Habibs I knew in Clarksburg. They were outgoing people with the gift of small talk that is an asset in merchandising. Their cousin was somber and deliberate; his English was carefully spoken but barely adequate for the serious thoughts that

23

he wanted to articulate. He had a sense of humor that flashed unexpectedly, but it brought only the slightest relaxation to the intensity of his personality.

His integrity gave him a forthright quality. He told me that he was a Christian, although his family was Muslim. When I asked if such conversions were not unusual, he conceded that they were but explained that in Lebanon, his home, his family kept the Bible and the Qur'an side by side and had not been upset by his becoming a Christian. The change in his life had happened when he was an undergraduate at AUB—the American University in Beirut. He was now working in a government hospital in Cairo and hoping to be admitted to a medical school in the United States.

"But I am not going to stay there after I get my M.D.," he said. "Too many people from the Middle East leave to study and never return. I will come back here to do the Lord's work."

I said I presumed that he would go to Lebanon.

"Not necessarily. It depends on conditions there."

"Does that mean you may come back to Egypt to practice medicine?"

He shrugged. "Perhaps. I do not know. Egypt is not my home. I am not Egyptian. Egyptians consider themselves different from the rest of us."

Those words are clear in my memory because they expressed a truth about the Middle East that was reinforced many times for me. Islam is a unifying force of great power in the Middle East, and so is pride in being an Arab. And yet there are conflicting loyalties—to family, tribe, and land—so ancient and elemental that they generate distrust and disdain of other Muslims or Arabs who are not of one's own circle. I hear Ali's words again whenever the news tells of gunfire or harsh words between Arab peoples.

That evening, of course, I had just begun to learn about the Middle East. So I asked what it meant to be an Arab. By my count, there were only two Arabs there, Miriam and Ali, and she was silent while he shrugged and grunted.

I looked at one and then the other. "You two are Christians. How does it feel to be Christians in a society that is overwhelmingly Muslim?"

"Mr. Smith," Angela Baker exclaimed with a laugh, "that is such a large question!"

"I guess it depends somewhat"—John raised one of his hands and rocked it like a little boat trying to stay afloat—"on whether you're an optimist or a pessimist about the Middle East. It isn't just a

24

religious question. I'm not sure there are strictly religious questions in the Middle East. When you ask about religion, you ask about politics, economics, culture, peace and justice—everything."

I was about to ask him to explain when Miriam interfered. I thought her words peremptory, but perhaps it was because she spoke in Arabic, intruding on our English. She seemed to address John. He frowned in concentration, then nodded when she had finished. He looked at me and smiled.

"Miriam likes to test my Arabic. She has observed that you now know something about each of us. She thinks that perhaps you would be kind enough to tell us something about yourself."

I looked at her and she met my eyes with a calm directness that was almost a challenge.

"There's not much to tell," I said cautiously. I recited my vital statistics, touched on Nancy's death, and talked a bit about my construction business. At that moment, the couple from Scandinavia excused themselves and Angela went with them to "settle the books." That left me with Ali, Miriam, and John as an audience, and, looking at them, I knew I couldn't put off the issue any longer.

I took my cue from Mr. Nakamura's comment about my search for Mary Salter: "Actually," I said, "I'm here partly on vacation and partly on an errand of mercy. . . ."

So I told them about my assignment. They were silent as they listened. I finally looked up and met Miriam's eyes again. She said, "You haven't told us her name."

"Mary Salter."

In the same flat tone she had used before, Miriam said, "I know her. A couple of years ago, she showed up here one night. She'd been in Turkey. But I remember what she was like and it doesn't match your description."

"What!" In my excitement, I upset my tea. "I can't believe it. Are you sure? She was a blonde, a rich-man's-daughter type, maybe on the moody side?"

Miriam remembered her as being blonde and ignored the rest of my question. When I suggested that Angela might know, she said Angela had been home on leave then.

"Do you know where she is now? Perhaps at the American University here?" I turned to John. "I think she might be interested in learning Arabic."

He shook his head. "I don't know anybody from the U.S. by that name."

"Well, I guess I've got my day cut out for me tomorrow," I said.

"Off to the American University. This is really amazing. Miriam, is there anything else . . .?"

But Ali interrupted me, saying that he had to be at the hospital early the next morning but would help me move to Nakamura's room right away if Angela said it was all right. She agreed and we made the move. I thought about talking with Miriam some more, but by that time it was after 11, so I decided to wait until morning.

Fatigue, jet lag, or the first stages of what hit me twenty-four hours later—whatever it was, I overslept the next morning and breakfasted by myself. I took a cab to the American University campus and spent about six hours making fruitless subtle inquiries of students. Ultimately, I gave up, found the Administration Office, and said point-blank that I was looking for a relative who was enrolled there. No luck. I walked back to Zamalek, on an afternoon that was as hot and close as an attic in August. A cool shower made me feel better, but I fell off to sleep and missed supper. No one was around when I came downstairs about 10 o'clock. I found flat bread, yellow cheese, and an orange in the refrigerator and went out on the front steps. I was peeling the orange when Miriam walked down the street into the light from our windows. It was good to see her and I asked her to join me. She hesitated and sat down. She was a very nice young woman, lithe in her movements and with a faint fragrance of flowers about her. I wished that she liked me, that we could be friends.

But I acted like a clod. I offered her a sticky section of peeled orange and declared, "Boy, have I had a nothing day."

Either my wish got to her or my low spirits, for her lips curved in a small, sympathetic smile—just for a moment. Encouraged, I elaborated on the day's futilities until, in mid-sentence, I realized that she had probably spent that day with people who had problems that made mine puny. "I beg your pardon," I said. "I'm acting like a jerk."

"There was one thing about the girl you're looking for." She spoke as if she had suddenly decided to offer me a clue. "I want to show you something. Can you wait a moment?"

I nodded dumbly, not knowing what to expect. She was back almost immediately with a paperback book and some pieces of paper. "That's her book," she said, handing it to me. "She left it here because she said others might like to read it. She was interested in Russian religion. From what you said, I don't think you know about that."

It was a little book, with bent, dirty corners. All I could make out

26

was the title, "The Way of the Pilgrim. Translated from the Russian."

"I read it. It's good." Miriam put the other papers in my hands—a dozen or so brochures and leaflets. "You asked about what I do with the garbage collectors and other things. These will tell you." Then, before I could say anything, and without even a "goodnight," she was gone.

I don't know how much longer it was before John showed up. I think that humans can absorb just so much; that's the way it is with me—after a point, I just tune out. So I'd been sitting there, holding the book and papers, thoughts and images tumbling endlessly in the air inside my head.

John sat down and lit his pipe. The flare of his lighter reflected on the book cover and served as a torch as we thumbed through the leaflets. Each was about a different type of church work. When I told him that Miriam had given them to me, he merely grunted and snapped out the lighter. I enjoyed talking about her, so I tried to pump him a little about her: yes, she was very nice; yes, they'd gone out together some; no, just friends. I got as far as asking where she came from and he said he thought her folks were in Lebanon then, or maybe Jordan. "Well, good night, Amon," he said cordially, clapped me on the shoulder and went inside.

The tumbling in my head had subsided, replaced by a monologue: Is something going on that I don't understand? Is Miriam covering up for Mary Salter? Is John the Swede covering up for Miriam? These are religious people and now I am told that Mary Salter, in addition to being a scatterbrain rich kid, a rebellious daughter, a frustrated girl friend, is also into Russian religion. Whom shall I believe? I feel the book and papers in my hand. When you hunt bear in the mountains, what track do you follow? The freshest, of course. I have fresh tracks in my hands. They are clues. Somewhere among the Christians in Cairo—never mind that a week ago you didn't even know there were Christians in Cairo—I may find Mary Salter. If she's here, I'll find her. I'll do it if I have to read every page in this book and go to every place in these pamphlets. . . .

"Resolutions grown late at night wither in the morning light." Yet what laid me low the next day was not a loss of ardor; my gastrointestinal system rebelled. I swallowed some Lomotil but I couldn't drag myself out of the house. About mid-morning Ali came by to ask how I was feeling. He had the morning off at the hospital and was staying home to study.

"Wait a minute," I said as he started to leave. "Remember what I told you about that young woman I'm looking for? I found out later from Miriam that she is interested in Russian religion."

He shrugged. "People study many things today."

"But what connection would that have with her coming to Egypt?"

"Maybe none. There was a time, back before the Revolution, when a lot of Russians—peasants—made pilgrimages to the Holy Land."

"That doesn't connect with Egypt."

"Egypt is not Jerusalem but do not forget that Our Lord and his family lived here when he was a small child. Christians have been in Egypt since the earliest days of the Church."

His deep-set eyes held me, seeking confirmation that I grasped the importance of what he was saying. I nodded and said, "I see." He sat down and leaned toward me.

"If this person is a sincere young lady . . . ." He started again: "If in her heart she would have a rich experience of faith, she could perhaps come to be of the Coptic Church. Do you understand what I am saying?"

"Perhaps. But can you help me?"

"Now you know me, I am now a Christian and was Muslim. I do not yet belong to one Christian church or another. These denominations and sects—sometimes they are angry with one another, so much that they don't have enough time to preach the Gospel."

"Same way at home."

"But you know, my friend, I am coming much to admire the Copts. They have survived so much, so long. They have suffered so much for their faith. Do you know that so many Christians— Christians of the East—I cannot begin to count them—were martyrs? Slaughter. Torture. They have been, as they say, 'baptized in tears.' And the Copts among them. And today, what do we find in Egypt? The Coptic Orthodox Church of about 5,000,000 people!"

I started to express my admiration, but he was too enthusiastic to let me interrupt.

"Once I met an American missionary," he continued, "and I told him this and he was very suspicious. Do you know what I said to him? I said I beg your pardon but the Coptic Orthodox Church is not senile or corrupt; it has been and is now—right now!—a true, alive force for Jesus Christ in the Middle East. He didn't know what to say. Then I told him about the Church's Christian education program, how well-trained the teachers are and the good literature that is produced for them. And finally I let him know how important offices in Egypt's new government are held by Coptic Christians and how the Church itself plays a big role in the life of the nation."

I could imagine this impassioned man telling somebody off and I chuckled. "What did he say to all that?"

"Oh, he was not a bad man. He just didn't understand. He was surprised when I told him the Coptic Church had missionaries working in Ireland long before the United States even existed. But I didn't want him to feel too bad. He is here to help us, is he not? Missionaries before—a hundred years or more—that's something else. They came over to convert Muslims. How many, one hundred, one thousand, maybe a few more, out of millions? But who they got instead were people from the churches that were already here. That's one reason why there are so many Christian churches in the Middle East. There are the ancient churches that were here from the beginning and then there are the churches made up of people whose ancestors left the old churches to help the missionaries start new ones."

"It sounds like quite a mixture. But the Copts came through okay?"

"You should see for yourself! There is a big Coptic cathedral here, St. Mark's, and every Friday night there is a Bible study. The Coptic pope speaks. Five or six thousand people come. That's tonight. You'll be better by that time. I'll take you!"

A Bible study? I hadn't been to a Bible study since I was fourteen. I squirmed. What was a pope doing in Cairo? I shook my head. "Thanks, Ali, but I don't feel . . . ."

"Another reason, another reason," he declared. "Your missing relative. If she is truly a young lady of faith, a Christian pilgrim, and is in Cairo, she may come. This is very big, very important in Cairo. Everybody knows about it and comes."

So? I might be under the same roof with Mary Salter? Five or six thousand people is quite a congregation, but it might be possible to detect a blonde pilgrim among all those devout Cairenes. "Okay," I said. "I'll go."

It was a wise decision, because, by the end of the day, I was itching to get out and do something. I'd spent a frustrating afternoon with the brochures and book that Miriam had given me. They were simple enough to read, but I tried to do more with them than read them. I looked on them as clues to Mary Salter. The more I thought about it, the more I persuaded myself that Miriam had given them to me to serve in that way.

Even before Ali dropped by to see me, I shuffled weakly around the halls hoping to bump into Miriam. I didn't find her so I went back

29

to my room, read the leaflets once before Ali arrived, and then got back to them later. I reread all the short stuff a couple of times and studied the illustrations with a magnifying glass I got from Ali. Most of it was about the Coptic Evangelical Church, which confused me, since I remembered that Ali had talked about the Coptic Orthodox Church. When I went to borrow the magnifying glass, I asked if there was a difference.

"Oh, yes," he said. "Coptic Evangelical Church is the result of long-time American missionary work in Egypt. They are fine people, they have close relations with Presbyterians in your country. But they are not the same as Coptic Orthodox. Sometimes the two churches work together, sometimes no."

I didn't understand entirely, but I didn't particularly care, so I went back to my attempts at detection, leaflet by leaflet.

Here was a publication title "Home Economics Program," illustrated by a photograph of a young woman knitting. No resemblance at all to the Mary Salter on the flickering movie screen in old Harry's office. I read about the Evangelicals' efforts in villages to help women learn needlework, knitting, home management, food preparation, nutrition, sewing, child care, and something called mothercraft. More than 2,300 women had taken the course. Not bad, but I couldn't see Mary Salter helping out with anything so domestic.

The next one, on literacy, seemed a possibility, since I had Mary pegged as a scholarly type. I read that in Egyptian villages illiteracy is likely to run as high as eighty-five per cent. The Coptic Evangelical Social Services agency teaches them to read, and then encourages them to read what they need to better their· lives. The leaflet contained quotations from people involved in the program, but there was no mention of Mary.

All together, I went through a dozen brochures: how to raise better chickens, learning to be a leader, on-the-spot medical attention, how to fatten cattle, raising bees, publishing books and magazines, sponsoring family life education as a means of raising healthier, happier families, and checking Egypt's crisis in population growth. All commendable, all without a hint of Mary Salter.

When I got through them, I found that Miriam had also given me a somewhat larger booklet on the Coptic Orthodox Church. I examined it, too, and discovered the Orthodox seemed to be neck-and-neck with the Evangelicals in providing social services. As Ali had mentioned, the Orthodox were particularly high on education. Still no clue of Mary.

The Pilgrim paperback was small and I read through it in hop, skip, and jump fashion. It's a kind of diary of a Russian man a century ago who walked across his homeland as a pilgrim to Jerusalem. He was on what could be called a spiritual quest. Eventually he took up what is called the Prayer of Jesus. This meant that over and over, all the time, he prayed, "Lord Jesus Christ, have mercy on me."

You end up liking the Pilgrim and appreciating his devotion. You realize that his Christianity, even if it's not one hundred per cent the same as the Christianity you're accustomed to, is the real thing.

At the back of the book there was a list of people, ancient leaders of the church, whom the Pilgrim refers to. The surprising thing was that these people were from the Middle East. Someone named Anthony the Great had been born in Egypt in about A.D. 250 Chrysostom, a name I'd run across someplace, was called "the most famous of the Greek fathers" but had been born in Syria about 345 A.D. Another one was John of Damascus; he was supposed to have been a great hymn writer and sure enough I remembered singing songs he'd written: "The Day of Resurrection" and "Come, ye faithful, raise the strain."

By the end of the afternoon, I was fretting over wasting a day. I was also beginning to feel a little uneasy and angry. Harry Salter had told me the kind of person his daughter was, and she seemed like somebody who needed to be dragged home. But ever since then, the more I learned about her, the more my conception of her changed.

*   *   *

John heard that Ali and I were going to the Bible study and invited himself along. I hoped that Miriam might come, too, but no one seemed to have an idea where she was.

Going to a Bible study wasn't my idea of a fun-filled evening, but things got interesting. St. Mark's Cathedral soars toward the sky, an immense concrete building of domes and arches. It dominates a walled-in compound of Coptic Orthodox structures, which, when we arrived in the cool early evening, was filling with people. They gathered in sociable small groups, many of them younger men and women, reminding me of how people back home stand around and talk after Sunday services in the summer.

When we went in, someone spotted us as visitors and took us down to the front row. From back to front, the sanctuary seemed as long as a football field and so high that I had to look carefully to make out pigeons wheeling in the darkness far overhead. Ali explained that the building was started in the 1960s and wasn't entirely finished yet. The walls were bare of any decoration and I could see marks of the wooden forms that had been used in construction. To my eye, its stark simplicity added to its grandeur.

I kept looking around for a blonde head. The auditorium was filling up, men sitting on one side, women on the other. I asked Ali whether he thought there might be any Muslims among so many people.

"Perhaps a few," he answered. "But as for Muslims becoming Christians or Christians becoming Muslims, that's something to be careful about. When someone wants to change from one to the other, the government insists that both religious groups be notified." Ali shrugged. "It's supposed to be fair for everybody, but in Egypt, where so many people are Muslim, it's easier for a Christian to become a Muslim than the other way around."

"That's true," John said. "The Egyptian parliament came close to passing a law that called for the death penalty for any Muslim converting to Christianity. President Sadat squelched it after Coptic Christians made a very strong protest."

Ali nodded. "Yes, well, you see, that may have been because some groups in Islam are very conservative. They think that Western influence is breaking down the Islamic way of life. They are real fanatics; they even assassinated a former Egyptian cabinet minister who opposed what they are trying to do."

"If that's the way things are," I told Ali, "I wouldn't be seen here if I were a Muslim."

He nodded, then raised a cautionary finger. "But my Egyptian friends, no matter what they are, really aren't trying to convert one another. The Egyptians are peaceful people. Sadat is trying to help relationships between Christians and Muslims. The great concern of Egyptians is survival. They don't have time for trying to get one another to convert."

"What happens when a Muslim man wants to marry a Christian woman, or vice versa?" I asked.

"Well, it's very hard."

While we had been talking, people had begun to take places on the platform at the front of the church. Half of them were clergy, bearded men dressed in long black robes and little round black hats. The other half were laymen in shirts and slacks, not wearing ties. A microphone was sitting on a small table and another floor microphone was in place behind it. Off to one side was a big chair with a canopy over it; I decided it might be the pope's throne.

It may have been, but when he came in, he didn't sit in it. There was a flurry of greetings when he arrived, including the kissing of his ring. He went about this business briskly and then sat down at the little table. The proceedings began with hymn-singing, led by a layman at the floor microphone. While this was going on—I didn't understand a word or recognize a tune—some of the congregation began to pass slips of paper forward. Ali informed me that the Pope often began his Bible studies by inviting his listeners to send him questions on which they wanted his comments. The singing lasted about ten or fifteen minutes and the Pope, whose name is Shenouda III, spent the time reading and sorting the questions. He was a stocky man, wearing black-rimmed spectacles, and his bare arms jutted out of the folds of his robe as he organized his work.

He read the first question, in Arabic, of course, and Ali translated it for me: a 22-year-old woman who was engaged to a 42-year-old man asked if it was all right to break the engagement. The Pope told her it would be better to break up than to marry and then try to get a divorce. In the next question, someone wanted to know whether it was best to be a monk or to get married and be a priest. The Pope advised the person to seek the counsel of his priest.

John leaned over to tell me that the Coptic clergy may be monks, who are celibate, or priests, who may marry. "Monasticism is very important in the life of the Coptic Orthodox," he said. "All the bishops are from monasteries. I understand that when he was called to be a bishop, Pope Shenouda had spent ten years in a monastery, eight of them living in solitude in a cave."

Ali came in at me from the other side. "Liturgy is also very important to the Copts. The Coptic liturgy contains all of the Bible story, so each time a person participates in the liturgy, he experiences the entire gospel message." He tapped my knee for emphasis. "Monasticism and the liturgy have helped the church survive."

After a time, the Pope put the questions aside and began a lecture. Ali's translation went something like this: Christians need to take care not to become loose in their faith, not to let their spiritual lives cool down. If you feel yourself cooling, he said, warm yourself by humbling yourself, by reminding yourself of God, by confessing, by spiritual reading, by prayer, by spiritual friendship. Remember strong Bible passages by writing them down, because you will need them when you are weak. If you want to walk in the way of God, you must seek perfection, a long, endless road. . . .

He talked for forty-five minutes. At first, he leaned forward on his table like a teacher speaking patiently to his students. Then he gained momentum and enthusiasm. He had no notes to refer to; I

33

guess he had stored up so much in that cave that his words could never exhaust the supply. His voice rose and fell and he pointed and gestured in rhythm with his sonorous Arabic.

When he was finished—and he stopped suddenly, seemingly because of time rather than lack of more to say—word was passed to us that he would be outside, giving communion. We slipped out into the darkness and stood in a circle of lamplight where a line of people quickly formed. The Pope and a small group of followers appeared out of another exit and passing us, he recognized us as strangers with a quick smile and nod. He began to pass out the bread. Each recipient kneeled as he or she took the fragment; there were alternate lines of men and women.

Suddenly, as we watched, a man stepped out of the shadows toward the Pope. He was instantly blocked by some of the church leaders. It was a tense moment of constraint and whispered argument. Ali listened and explained to me, "He wants to present a petition. They have told him, after all have been served." The man stood aside, waited, and finally was allowed to go forward with his paper. The Pope moved closer to the light and held the paper up to its glow while the petitioner watched, hands knotted at his sides. He was a young man, slight, bare-headed, in shirtsleeves, waiting as if his life hung in the balance. It seemed to me then, and does now, a liturgy all its own, a living drama of the hope and expectancy, the reverence and faith that have kept Christianity alive in the Middle East across all the years of tortured witness.

The Pope nodded, motioned to one of his assistants, called the young man over, and they conferred. When they were done, he raised an arm in a quick gesture combining benediction and farewell and left in a car waiting in the adjoining courtyard.

When we got back to Church House, the three of us made scrambled eggs. I admitted that I'd had a better time than I had expected. "You know, the Egyptians—it's great how friendly they are. Even on that bus coming home, jammed in among a lot of people, I didn't feel at all like a stranger. Yet, in spite of that and being safe on the streets, I see a lot of soldiers around, carrying arms."

"Oh, that is because of national security," Ali explained. "You know, this country has been in a state of war with Israel for thirty years. Other Arab countries, too. Everyone stays ready for war. It makes life hard. There is not enough money to do things that will make life better for people." He winked at John and said, "It even is not too pleasant for American tourists who try to take pictures of bridges."

34

As we were laughing, Angela Baker arrived. She sat down with us and accepted a cup of tea while we told her about our evening.

"Just before you came in," I said, "Ali was reminding me how hard it is for Egypt and other Arab countries to be ready for war all the time."

She nodded and answered in her hearty way, "I'm sure it's a burden on the Israelis as well."

She had given the conversation a turn that provided me an opportunity.

"You know," I said "I haven't talked much about why I'm here, looking for Mary Salter." I really don't want to bother you with it. But it's on my mind, of course, and now we're talking about Israel, where she's supposed to have this boy friend."

I looked around at them, but no one said anything. They were just listening, eyes on something else.

"But I don't want to go there, if she's here. Obviously. And I think she is. The reason I think so is because of Miriam. She's said and done things that make me feel that Mary Salter is here. I almost have a sense that she wants me to know. Only for some reason, she can't get it out."

My three friends were still silent, but Angela was looking at me. I spoke directly to her. "Perhaps Miriam would be able to tell me if she and I were better friends. But my problem is, how do I make friends with an Arab woman? Can I ask her out to a movie? Or would it be better if someone suggested that she might be my guide and take me out to see the Pyramids and the Sphinx? I mean, could one of you do that?"

There was a discouraging silence and I thought I'd gone too far. "Let's forget . . . ."

Angela interrupted me. "Well, actually, either would be all right. But the problem is that Miriam has left. She's gone to Lebanon. She's been wanting to visit her family there for some time and she learned the other day that she could get away from her work for a while. So I'm afraid she can't help you."

For a few minutes, I didn't know what to say. Ali and John took up the slack in conversation. Finally I asked when Miriam might be coming back. Angela responded that she expected to stay in Beirut for several weeks.

We cleaned up the dishes and then I excused myself. I went up to my room and walked through its darkness to the little balcony looking out on Peter and Paul Street. The evening had suddenly turned sour. I was tired, discouraged, frustrated. I slumped in the old

35

wicker rocker and, after a while, I began to doze. Finally, I got up to go to bed. The note fell at my feet when I pulled down the sheet. The old-fashioned, clear-glass lightbulb flared on the small sheet and the short, strong lines of handwriting:

"I'm sorry to say goodbye this way. I hope you read the book. You may keep it. Enjoy your visit to Cairo and please do not be too disappointed if you do not find what you are looking for."

It was signed, "M."

I shook my head, punchdrunk. Not only had she run out on me, but she was telling me to forget about finding Mary Salter. That's right, she was telling me—not hinting at it or suggesting or implying. Miriam, for a modest Middle Eastern maiden, you speak your mind, don't you?

Her handwriting—clear lines with the backslant angle that left-handed people give to their script. Where had I seen writing like that before? Why had it stuck in my mind?

And then it came to me, the memory of light, a pool of brightness lying across an old man's desk, in a room whose darkness was not the curtain of the gentle Egyptian night but of a lashing West Virginia rainstorm.

CHAPTER
THREE

O NCE I was aboard the plane to Lebanon, I had time to reflect on the sanity of what I was doing. The reflection was not reassuring.

In the clear light of day at 20,000 feet, all I had to go on was a half pint of evidence that Miriam seemed to know Mary Salter, maybe even to act like her, and to write left-handed, as Mary did. Back in his office in Clarksburg, Harry Salter had Xeroxed and given me a copy of the letter his daughter had written him. When I had first compared it with the note left me by Miriam, I thought I found likenesses: an independence of tone and a peculiar slant and shaping of script. Now I wasn't so sure.

The flight was short. We came in over Beirut from the sea, the beautiful blue-green Mediterranean curling up toward a modern city that had been sculpted on the slopes of lofty coastal mountains. My friend the travel agent had tried to discourage me from getting a visa for Lebanon because of the Israeli attack in the south three or four months earlier, but when I looked down at it casually now, I saw only serenity.

A bus brought us from the plane to the arrivals building, and once again there were troops, three big black men wearing light blue berets. *Hah,* I thought, *Fijians in the UN contingent that is here to get things back to normal in the south.* I felt that they were a kind of international police force, *our* international force, and coupled with the sight of modern Beirut, they gave me a sense of arriving at a comfortable respite from the turbulence of Cairo.

So I had no premonition of anything wrong. Checking through customs was a dog-eat-dog affair and welcomers who waited for passengers were pressing against barriers, waving, shouting, and pointing. I concluded that the Lebanese must be a volatile and emotional people. But I was surprised when I passed through the building and found more barriers and more excited people lined up outside.

A middle-aged, red-faced man appeared at my side and asked me, in a gravelly British accent, if I were interested in sharing a cab to the city. I assented and he quickly found one.

"Where are you staying?" he demanded.

"The Maryland, I hope," I responded, thankful at remembering the travel agent's reluctant suggestion.

Inside and under way, my companion said, "I'm stopping there, too. Good thing. It's in Ras Beirut. You couldn't have made it to the other side."

"Why not?"

Bushy eyebrows, arched high, assailed me. "You haven't heard? Fighting again."

The cab slowed and I squinted ahead through the sunglare on the windshield. Soldiers at a checkpoint: a sand-bagged shelter with a twin-barreled anti-aircraft gun squatting next to it.

We stopped and a hawk-nosed, brown-faced corporal gave us a quick appraisal before waving us on. Arabic flowed between front seat and back and the Englishman said, "Those were Syrians—part of the Arab League's peace-keeping force. Incidentally, we're taking a detour to avoid the shelling."

We sped along a road toward the late afternoon sun, looking at fields and a garbage dump. The driver took a couple of quick glances to his right, raised his arm, and made a comment. The Englishman said, "Oh?" We stared toward the north and there, indeed, lying close to the distant ground, the black smoke hung. "That's where it is," he said. I nodded, but I think we both had a hard time believing it.

"Who's fighting?" I inquired.

"I gather it's some of the Syrians and the right-wing militia," the

38

Englishman said. *because of detour?*

We ultimately turned right, briefly followed a seaside avenue, and then entered the city's business district. There was an air of normality here among small, modern shops and glass-fronted restaurants. The Maryland stood at a quiet corner; we were welcomed by a soft-voiced desk clerk.

"Oh, sir," he said in answer to my query, "there is no shortage of rooms these days."

The Englishman was Ian Yorke, a UN agricultural specialist who was in the Middle East trying to track down a livestock virus. We had dinner together.

"Doomed country, this," he growled at me. "Too little, smaller than your Connecticut. Maybe 3,000,000 people, although there's been no census for nearly fifty years, political reasons. Quite a history, going all the way back to the Phoenicians, trade and all that. After World War II, Arab and European countries used it as a commerce and financial center, place to invest oil money and to have a good time, a cultural site. Lovely then, if you had money.

"But it was a fragile place. Most of that wealth came from other countries, not from what Lebanon could produce. The money stayed in Beirut, the rest of the country didn't see much of it. Economic injustice. Political injustice. One-tenth of the population got one-half of the money. Then inflation, hitting the middle class hardest of all. The poor people from the farm land coming to the cities for jobs that weren't there. How about that for an explosive combo? And then what happened?"

He rapped a knuckle twice on the table and glared at me. "Palestinians. People displaced from their homes by the fighting with Israel. Ending up in Lebanon, looking for a temporary place to stay. Living here, influencing the government, which already had more headaches than it could handle. Some of them using the camps to stage attacks on Israel. Do you know that as many as 400,000 Palestinians are in Lebanon now? That throws everything out of balance. In this country, government is supposed to be nicely teetering on so many Christians, so many Muslims, so many everything else. And the result? All the big boys are using little Lebanon in a new way. It's a battlefield now."

At that point, he grumbled into silence. I finished my coffee and proposed that we take an evening stroll. He murmured an assent and we signed our bills and climbed the stairs to the lobby. We had reached the pavement outside when the desk clerk came solicitously out behind us: "Lovely evening though it is, gentlemen, the

39

management suggests that guests stay indoors because of the present uncertain conditions."

Yorke said he was going to bed, so we parted. I strolled restlessly around the lobby, looking at the English hunting prints, until I realized I could be putting the time to better use. The clerk assured me that the telephones were working, even across the line dividing the city. So I spent the next hour calling listings for the name Assad. I had no luck whatsoever: some people didn't answer, some spoke only Arabic or French, and the three who understood my English had no relations named Miriam. What next? If there was a Coptic Orthodox church in the city, perhaps someone there would know of her. I checked the phone book again; no luck. When I asked the desk clerk, he shook his head and suggested that I wait until the next day and inquire about churches at the government tourist agency.

In the morning, I tried to get news on the radio but there was nothing in English. An occasional pedestrian strolled past the lobby windows; when the day man at the desk said good morning without warning me to stay off the streets, I ventured outside. A cab was parked at the curb and the driver looked at me inquiringly. I told him I wanted to find a Coptic Orthodox church but he didn't understand me. He shook his head but then, as an afterthought, said there was some kind of Christian office a block or two up the street: could he take me there? I sympathized with his eagerness for a fare, but I felt like walking.

The street was narrow and sunlit, through a section of shops, walled gardens, and large private homes. Bouquets of flowers cascaded onto the sidewalk in front of a florist's and, at a corner, a smiling boy was selling fruits along a fence of ornate ironwork.

I almost missed the place I was looking for. The cab driver had told me there was a sign with a cross on it. What I finally found was a simple wooden placard, white on blue, bearing the words, "The Net." The cross had been worked into the lettering, making the "t" in the word "net." The building itself seemed to be partly a business address and partly a small apartment house.

Obeying a directory in the vestibule, I took a tiny, creaking elevator to the fifth floor.

There was an invitation to enter on the double door, but the door was locked. I rapped and waited but no one answered. After a few minutes, I gave up and started down the stairs, too annoyed to summon the elevator. On the second landing down, I came upon a boy and a girl, twelve or thirteen years old, kicking a soccer ball to one another. When I told them what I was doing there, the boy began kicking the ball again. "Sunday," he said. "Closed."

Well, he could have kicked me, too. I'd forgotten what day it was. While I stood there, berating myself, a man about my own age came up the stairs. The kids greeted him in Arabic and the girl pointed at me while he was still talking. The man put out his hand and smiled.

"Hello. I belong to Net. My friends here say you were trying to get in."

His name was Yusuf Nasar. I told him I had come by to inquire about a church in Beirut and started to explain about looking for a relative. He interrupted when he identified my accent as American; he'd won a degree in economics from a Canadian university. Would I have coffee with him?

He talked from his apartment's kitchenette as I surveyed the pleasant jumble of sunbrightened buildings from a tiny balcony. His wife and small daughter were staying with her family in Tripoli because of conditions in Beirut.

"You feel it's dangerous then?"

"Well, I'm scared," he said matter-of-factly. "Things aren't as bad here as they are on the other side of the city, but you could get killed."

I looked again at the quiet street below. "That's hard to believe. How do you put up with it?"

"What else can we do? It's our country. Some people lose hope and go. Others of us stay. We got through the fighting in '75 and '76. We were lucky. Forty thousand people were killed. Afterwards, we began to think that things were getting better. But now it's started again. We were getting accustomed to quiet times, that's what makes it hard."

He sighed and said, "Well, that church you would like to find—I'm not sure about it, but, if you'd like to have me help you, perhaps we can find out tomorrow."

"Great. I don't know what I would have done if I hadn't met you. I just took a chance, coming here. What is The Net, anyway?"

He laughed and made a small, deprecating gesture. "Well, the name isn't much, is it? Some of us thought we should have a name and that's the best we could do. Actually, we're just a group of people, Christians of a lot of different kinds, who have a commitment to the same idea. It's a sort of lay ecumenical thing. We all believe in the unity of the church of Jesus Christ. We got started about ten years ago when a few of us met at an ecumenical work

41

camp in France. Three men and a woman, all from Arab countries. They were from different nations and different churches, but they realized—they came to a kind of sudden, shared insight—that they were all one in Christ. So they kept in touch afterward and each of them got a few friends interested in the idea. Someone thought they should have a newsletter, and once that was started, we realized we were sort of a society or movement. It's pretty loose and flexible, but we're tied together, too, by wanting to bring our churches and our nations closer together. That's why we call ourselves—and our newsletter—The Net."

"You must be doing all right, if you have your own office. I thought you were going to tell me that you get your name from the Bible. One of the verses I remember is the one in which Jesus says, 'Follow me, and I will make you fishers of men.' "

Nasar laughed. "Hey, you're right. We did have that in mind, too. Maybe you should be one of us. We're mostly younger people."

"Well, I don't think . . ." I started to say, and then interrupted myself, suddenly realizing the implication in his words. I took a shot in the dark: "How large is Net in Beirut? You wouldn't know a family named Assad, would you? It's their daughter, Miriam, who I'm really trying to get in touch with."

His eyebrows went up and he opened his hands toward me. "I know of Miriam Assad. She is a friend of my sister-in-law. I thought she was out of the country. Yes, her people could be in Net. Is she your relative?"

"Mary Salter is my relative's name. I'm looking for Miriam because she may know where Mary is."

"If Miriam has returned, she will be with her family. How important is it that you get in touch with her today?"

"Well—" I shrugged. "At least I'd like to talk with her. Do you know her family's address? I'll get a ride."

He shook his head. "No. Not possible. The Assads live on the east side."

I looked at him and the morning seemed to lose its brilliance. "How bad is that?"

He shook his head. "We can't tell, really, but bad enough. Radio reports aren't reliable. We could call on the phone if we have to, but when people are having trouble, you do not want to interfere. . . ."

I nodded. There was nothing I could say. When we finished the coffee, he said that he had work to do for the rest of the morning but that he was going swimming in the afternoon. Would I like to come?

"Swimming? Sure, great. Never been in the Mediterranean. But is it safe?"

"It's as safe as being on the street," he told me.

That afternoon was unreal. We swam, sun-bathed, drank soda, talked, looked at the girls, dozed a little—and two miles away men were sighting mortars in on enemy strong points. People of all ages were on the beach and the pleasant flow of the afternoon hesitated only once, when a single explosion boomed faintly in the distance. For a second or two, only the sea moved and only its sounds were heard.

I found out that Nasar was working on a special reconstruction project for an international relief agency. After graduation, he'd returned to Lebanon. By that time, his mother and father, with his two sisters, had moved to Turkey, where his father was a partner in an accounting firm. Yusuf told me he had paid them lengthy visits on two or three occasions.

That news gave me an opening that I tried to handle subtly. Without asking him directly, I wanted to know if Miriam Assad had been in Turkey, too. I asked him if he felt like a stranger when he was in Turkey.

"No, no more than anywhere else I've been. My family was there."

I told him about Mrs. Merkosian at home. "She was Armenian Orthodox and I got the impression from her that Christians in Turkey are at a disadvantage in a culture where Islam is so dominant. She said they really are in a minority situation."

"That's the truth. Long ago, of course, Istanbul was Constantinople, the capital of the Eastern Roman Empire and so significant in Christianity that it was called 'New Rome.' Even today, it is an important center for Eastern Orthodox churches. But, indeed, Christians are very much in the minority. Perhaps there are 200,000 of them—mostly Syrian Orthodox, as our family is, Armenian Orthodox, or Greek Orthodox—in a population of 41 million. One problem is getting a good education when you're young, because of tricky politics, social problems, and inflation. There are lots of other things, too, that need attention: better interfaith relations, better relations between the Christian groups, too, and issues relating to everything from economics to ecology."

I told him he seemed to know a good deal about the country and church activities there. He laughed and commented, "Oh, I am interested in both. Besides, one of my father's accounts is Redhouse Press, a publishing company in Istanbul supported by Christians in the United States. They do a Turkish dictionary that's the best thing of its kind. And the same group of American churches is very active in Turkish secondary schools, too."

"I flew over Turkey, coming from the States. The country looks different from the air than Egypt or Lebanon."

"It's different from the Arab world in many ways, even though Islam is so strong. Arabs were ruled by the Ottoman Turks for years, remember. It wasn't a happy time. There are Arabs who blame the Turks for the underdevelopment of some areas in the Middle East now."

He paused, as if he had no more to say about Turkey, so I asked him outright: "I'm not sure, but I may have heard that Miriam Assad has been there."

"Oh, yeah? That's news to me."

He gave me a quick, appraising glance. "How would you like to have a look around Beirut?" he asked.

We dressed and got into his little Fiat. "Things seem quieter now," he commented as we angled away from the beach, "but I don't know how far we can go."

The little car scooted up a steep road, winding among modern hotels and apartment buildings that looked down on the Mediterranean. Abruptly, we turned toward an area that, from a distance, I took to be a big construction site. I stared ahead at it idly until I saw the vacant windows, the scorched smear of dead fires, and the broken walls and the holes punched by gun and rocket fire.

Slowing down, Yusuf said, "This is the edge of the line. I'm going to stop here because to go farther would be dangerous."

He pulled up in front of the massive concrete corpse of a hotel. We got out, alone in the deserted neighborhood except for a small group of men on a street corner fifty yards away.

"This used to be the Holiday Inn," Yusuf said. "Ah, someone wants to find out about us."

Two young men, dressed in civilian clothes, came across the street casually. Yusuf greeted them with a little wave and offered them cigarettes. Not wanting to stare, I busied myself rubber-necking at the ruins around us. The three of them chatted amiably in Arabic and finally I asked Yusuf if I might take a picture.

"Sure," he answered, "but then let's go."

Once we were moving again, he told me that our visitors had been members of a militia group. "Not bad guys," he commented. "They're fair and they keep an eye on things."

"I don't understand this militia business," I told him.

He explained to me that there were a number of armed political groups in Beirut, each controlling a piece of territory. In the city where we were, the groups could be leftist, Palestine Liberation Organization, or Lebanese Muslim. Over in East Beirut, the Falangists—who were mostly Maronites—were in charge. The Syrian occupation troops, which the Arab League had asked to keep order after the fighting two years ago, were trying to get the Falangists to give up their weapons. But they didn't want to. That's what the fighting was supposed to be about.

"Maronites are Christians, right?" I asked. "In the papers back home, the headlines usually say that the Christians are fighting the Syrians."

"That's misleading. The groups fighting with the Syrians are Falangists or rightists. As I said, most of the people who belong to those political groups are Maronites. But the political groups aren't secular wings of the Maronite Church. It's not unusual for church leaders and the political leaders to disagree.

"You have to realize," he continued, "that the Maronites have their own tradition, a special history quite different from the rest of us. Their church was founded at the end of the fourth century and Maronites have maintained its identity and independence ever since, although they also have kept strong ties with the Roman Catholic Church. Persecution forced them to flee into the Lebanese mountains, but they survived and became strong. Today, they're the largest single group of Christians in Lebanon. They are also sometimes very proud about their religion and act as if it is superior to what other church people believe. But despite their prominence, they still represent only forty or forty-five percent of the total Christian population. There are lots of other Christians in Lebanon—Armenian Orthodox, Greek Orthodox, Syrian Orthodox, Greek Catholic, those are the main ones."

"I get the idea," I said. "But how come so many of the Maronites are involved in the Falange, and in the fighting?"

"The government here is supposed to preserve a balance of power between Christians and Muslims. The office of president is reserved for a Christian, the office of prime minister for a Muslim, and so on, all down the line. The president traditionally is a Maronite because the Maronites are the largest Christian church. But now, with the whole country upset, a lot of the Maronites are afraid they're going to lose that power."

Remembering Ian Yorke, I said, "Someone told me there's social unrest—I mean, aside from the fighting."

"That's the truth, that's part of it. A lot of money that came into the country when times were good stuck with big business people and bankers. Other Lebanese resent that. But really, the whole political arrangement is at fault. Political power is supposed to reflect population, okay? In the beginning, Christians and Muslims were roughly equal in number, so the offices were equally divided. But now, just about everyone who's honest about it, realizes that there are more Muslims than Christians. To me, it's not right that a Maronite be president just because he's a Maronite."

"So the fighting is going on over who is going to be in control. . . ."

"And because the Arab peace-keeping forces, mostly Syrian, say that there can't be any peace in Lebanon when individual groups maintain their own private armies." He sighed. "On the other side, some people think the Syrians just want to take over the whole country. Lebanon was part of Syria at one time, you know."

He'd been driving along the seacoast again, heading south. "Now let me show you something else," he said. "It won't make things any simpler or nicer."

The outskirts of Beirut were like those of American cities, highways clustered with stores, garages, houses, small industry, all mixed together. Our road's setting was softened on one side by the placid stretch of beach and sea. But that softness had been erased at the place where Yusuf pulled off the pavement.

"Maybe you'll want a picture of this," he said.

For a hundred yards or so, more ruins stretched before me. It was a humbler destruction that we had visited within the city: a scar of wrecked small buildings—crumbled walls and collapsed roofs hung with the viscera of broken plumbing and sagging power lines.

"Last spring, some PLO raided Israel from the sea and killed civilians near Tel Aviv. This is what happened in retaliation. Israeli intelligence was told that PLO members lived here. So their jets came over in a strike. This is what they did."

He got out with me and we picked our way to a spot where I could take a photo. As I was focusing, a man and a woman with a small child came out of a small cement structure that was still standing. Yusuf talked with them and, when I was finished, waved me over. "These people are still living here," he said. "As you can see, they have not recovered from what happened."

I suppose the adults were in their forties, dressed in a pick-up way in Western clothes. The little girl clung to her mother and both parents had a restrained, absent look as they shook hands.

"This is all they have left," Yusuf said quietly. "Their fourteen-

46

year-old daughter was killed."

When we were back in his car and on the road, he added, "When the planes came over, they ran for cover. The father had both the girls by the hand. A bomb exploded and the oldest was hit."

We were silent for a while. My mind finally came to rest on something that I could talk about.

"I guess I understand now, maybe a little, the spot you're in. Lebanon has plenty of problems of its own, but you're also caught in the crossfire between the Palestinians and the Israelis."

"That is right," Yusuf said. "That is a great reason why there must be peace and justice between Israel and the Palestinians. If not, Lebanon will die. It is dying now."

After a while, when we were further from the city, he showed me places along the shore where hotels and villas made impressive silhouettes against the flaming sunset.

"Before the war, they were filled with vacationers. Now they've been taken over by refugee families."

"Pretty nice places to stay, but what do they do about food and earning a living?"

"Oh, most of them figure something out. They start a little roadside stand or find an empty doorway in the city where they can sell pens or watches or something. My agency provides aid with what we have. And the churches, too. Some of the kids from the colleges—American University, for example—help out when they can."

As a second thought, he added, "Your relative wouldn't be going to school here, would she? Coming home from church this morning, just before I met you, I passed a campus tennis court and there were a couple of blondes there who looked like American types."

I asked if he knew their names and he reminded me he was a married man. It was mild humor, but worth a laugh on a sober evening. At the same time, I resolved to visit the universities the next day.

* * *

With a single exception, however, the events of the next day were quite beyond my control. I arose early and was walking up the street to the Net office when I saw Yusuf's Fiat turn out of the drive and accelerate toward me. He stopped when he saw me and stuck his head out of the window.

"Going to Sidon. Picking up Miriam Assad and somebody else. Want to come?"

"Sure." So much for shaping my day. I got in and we were off with a roar.

Yusuf had received a call early that morning telling him that some people in The Net wanted to meet to discuss the outbreak of fighting. They were eager to obtain first-hand information about East Beirut and had arranged for a member who was living there—a woman—to get out of the embattled area. She was bringing Miriam with her. They had a ride that would take them out of the city on the other side, then south, and finally, hopefully, west to Sidon. When he heard that they needed transportation from there to Beirut, Yusuf had volunteered.

"My office has some construction work in that area that I can look in on at the same time," he explained to me.

"How often do you get involved in these Net things?" I asked.

"Oh, on and off," he answered. "There's a kind of steering committee that meets once a month and some other people do the newsletter. Beyond that, we tend to work in groups of two or three people, or even independently, doing what we can in our churches or where we live and have our jobs. The meeting that's been called for this week is something special. The situation here is terrible. We've got to see if we can do something about it."

A blunt question came to my mind but I tried to state it politely. "Yusuf, is there really anything you can do? Even with the best intentions, what can a group like The Net accomplish?"

He was silent for a moment, looking at the road ahead. Finally, he said, "From one point of view, perhaps very little. Maybe feed a few people, find them places to live if their houses are destroyed, comfort them if they are hurt or if they are grieving because someone they love has been killed. Maybe speak a word of peace and forgiveness where we have influence as a group or as individuals. Perhaps merely be a symbol, a Net that embraces all—Orthodox, Assyrian, Catholic, Anglicans, and Protestants—to keep alive the hope of unity in our divided country."

It was my turn to be silent, thinking. After a while, I asked the name of the woman with whom Miriam was coming.

"Helena Tarazi," he answered. "She's a teacher. She's particularly interested in women's activities, in the churches and in society generally."

"How does it happen that Miriam is with her?"

"I don't know. Perhaps it has something to do with her family. Maybe they want her to return to Egypt."

In a half hour or so, we stopped at a village where Yusuf's agency

48

was building a clinic. A wedding was being celebrated, however, and no work was being done. We drank some sweet tea in honor of the bride and groom and left as quickly as good manners permitted.

I was interested in the countryside and saw banana plants and corn when the road turned inland and then, as we curved back toward the sea, admired the long, sandy beaches and the limitless blue-green margin of the sea.

"I've been trying to think why Sidon seems so familiar a name," I said.

"You remember Tyre and Sidon in the Bible," he told me. "We are traveling now where Jesus traveled."

So, once again, as in Egypt, this was land where he had been. I tried to comprehend.

After a while, Yusuf asked, "What do you think Miriam will say when she sees you?"

"I don't know. She's never been particularly happy to see me before." Then I told him bluntly what I felt: "I may be about to make a fool of myself. A very big fool."

I think he was about to ask what I meant, but just then we came over a hill and saw a town ahead of us. "Sidon?" I asked, and he nodded. An important place for centuries, he said. He pointed to an old stone fort thrusting out into the Mediterranean, and told me its foundations had been laid by the Phoenicians.

Yusuf's instructions were to meet the two women at a Greek Catholic orphanage on the hills overlooking the city. We had only reached the end of the fortress causeway, however, when I saw Miriam. She had just come out of a house half a block away and was walking toward us, alone.

"Stop," I said. I knew what I had to do. "Would you do me a favor? Miriam is over there. I want to talk with her alone. Could you go up and get the other woman and then come back and pick us up? We'll meet you over there, at that old castle. This sounds crazy, Yusuf, but I'm afraid if I don't take care of something right now, it'll never get done."

What a guy. He looked at her and then at me; he was puzzled but he grinned and shook his head. "Wow!" he said, and took off. He tooted as he passed Miriam and I knew from the way she stopped and stared after him that she recognized him and wondered about it. As she turned to continue, she saw me trudging across the street toward her.

I didn't know what she might do. Her step faltered for an instant but then she simply waited for me to reach her.

49

"Well, hello," she said. And she smiled. A surprised, delighted smile, as if I were an old friend she hadn't seen for a long, long time.

We walked across the rough stones to the fortress, the sea breeze tugging at us. Inside, there was a low wall, and we stopped to watch the waves washing against the rocks. She pushed her sunglasses up on her hair and looked at me.

"Are you okay?" I asked.

"Yes. And you?"

"I feel terrific. I didn't know what you were going to do when you saw me."

"I suppose not. I felt the same way when you showed up in the middle of the night in Cairo."

I let that sink in. Her eyes were blue, which I should have noticed before. Otherwise, with those black, short curls, the tanned skin, the Arabic, she could have been Egyptian, Lebanese, Syrian, almost anyone Mediterranean.

"You were safe. You had me fooled, the way you looked, the way you acted, everything. You dyed your hair and you learned Arabic, right? But what about your family in Beirut?"

"Oh, they're my adopted family. I met them when I was at AUB and make my home with them when I'm there. Their name is Assad, and I took it for use over here because I love them. And because I wanted to be a part of life here. That's why I'm Miriam, which is an Arabic way of saying Mary."

"You make it sound so simple. It worked beautifully. You're not the person I expected you to be."

She nodded and looked away as if her thoughts were momentarily elsewhere. Then she raised her eyes again in the direct way she had and said, "Once again, I can say the same thing. I can remember that time years ago when we had that party at my parents' house for Vietnam veterans and you came. You still look the same but I think you're different."

"What do they say, 'I can still work all day and dance all night'?"

She seemed to reflect a moment and then, laughing, said, "It's been a long time since I've heard that kind of talk."

Voices behind us made us turn. Yusuf was calling to us: "We're ready to go."

He'd borrowed a luggage rack at the orphanage and the little Fiat looked top-heavy with Miriam's and Helena Tarazi's suitcases. Helena was napping in the front seat when we came up. Even though fatigue showed in her face and movements, she was a tall and handsome woman.

Both women gave accounts of recent days in East Beirut: Falangists and Syrians alike were determined to win their objectives, at the cost of other people's lives and property as well as their own.

Yusuf made a vague attempt to find out what had happened between Miriam and me. I left the response to her and she didn't say much, except to remark how surprised she'd been to see me. Arriving earlier than expected in Sidon, she'd come down to the center of town to inquire about the health of an old man in the Assad family.

We stopped for a meal of kebab and hummus and flat bread at a roadside restaurant. At first we were restless, unwinding after the morning's tensions, but gradually a sense of peacefulness and friendship seemed to settle among us. Yusuf had a limitless supply of stories for our entertainment. Boasting of Middle Eastern culture, he told us a tale of the fortress in Sidon: how centuries ago a princess had sailed westward from it, never to be heard from again, and how her brother, going out to look for her, had come upon land at the far end of the Mediterranean and had first called it by the name we know today—his lost sister's name—Europa. And when I asked him if that legend were really true, he professed that it was but warned me, all the same, to be wary of Middle Eastern conversation.

"We Arabs are great talkers," he declared. "There is a story we tell of an old man whose nap was disturbed by noisy children. To get rid of them, he said that a wedding was taking place on the other side of the mountain and that everyone who went to it would get delicious things to eat—fruits and all kinds of sweets. He made it sound so good that the children all went running to get there. He was about to lie down again when he thought, such a wonderful wedding, I shouldn't miss it myself, and off he trotted after them."

I was glad our conversation ran this easy way, because I was preoccupied with Miriam and with what had been left unsaid between us. In times past, I had seen myself finding her and telling her, "I'm from your father. He sent me to bring you home." But now, sitting in her presence, listening to what she said and how she said it, looking at her as much as I could without staring, there seemed so much to be communicated between us that I didn't know how to start. It was puzzling, for I wasn't accustomed to being at a loss for words or reluctant about speaking my mind.

We ended the meal with Turkish coffee and started on the road back to Beirut. We made good time the first forty-five minutes or so, but after we passed the first Syrian checkpoint on the outskirts of the city, Yusuf remarked that the traffic was heavier than usual for a Monday afternoon. Both lanes toward Beirut carried a steady flow of

51

vehicles. Finally we were forced to a full stop. It was then we heard the explosions.

"At it again," Yusuf said, and reached to turn on the radio.

Five minutes later, we were moving at a crawl. The booming was louder now and more frequent. Smoke lay in the distance beyond the crests of the low hills to our right. Tiny figures stood on rooftops and on the ridged horizon, motionless, backs to us, intent on whatever they were watching. . . .

An announcement on the radio that I do not understand. Helena exclaims something in Arabic. Yusuf tries to tune the radio more precisely. "Beirut is burning," he announces.

Now the traffic is crawling stop-and-go, bumper to bumper. We are passing through the area bombed by the Israeli jets. In the late afternoon heat—from the sun and the idling motors—all car windows are down and passengers strain forward to hear radio announcements and to look ahead at the choked traffic and to the right at the threatening smoke.

Another report on the radio. Miriam translates: "He is saying the firing is heavier than yesterday." The traffic is so thick that some cars churned across the sandy island—one is desperately stuck—into lanes for traffic going the other way. I can imagine a head-on collision, flaming cars.

Now men in uniform—police or soldiers—are among us, trying to direct traffic. And people gather in front of the shops and houses along the highway, staring at our disordered, lock-step flight toward home or whatever other hiding place we think we have. Our anxiety mounts, fear trips anger. In the lane next to us, two cars, full of people, jockey for position. The drivers shout through open windows, curse, passengers join in, someone spits at a howling face, doors fly open, fists swing. We're about to be caught in a riot. . . .

But then we reached the bottleneck, the juncture of the road to the airport. An apoplectic policeman struggled to untangle the mess and we were suddenly free of it. Moments later, we turned along the seaside avenue, in among the shops, and Yusuf pulled up at my hotel.

I hesitated as I opened the car door. "Is there any way we can get together this evening?" The three of them thought not. I looked directly at Miriam. "I really need to talk to you. Perhaps in an hour or two. . . ."

"Tomorrow will be better," she told me. "I'll call you later."

I took a shower and then ordered dinner from room service. Harry Salter owed me that as a bonus for finding his daughter that day. I wondered if he would recognize her and what he would have

52

said to her if he had met her as I had. What would she have said to him? Did she speak to me as if I were he? Was that why she was nice to me, because she, in spite of everything between them, was a loving daughter and saw me as her father's agent, indeed almost as her father? A depressing thought to have in a lonely room, eating a lonely meal.

The phone rang at about 10:10. Her voice was tired. I told her I'd been thinking about her and she responded that she was sorry, that she realized she had made things difficult for me.

"It's not that," I protested. "Miriam—Mary—you see, I don't even know what to call you. How soon may I see you? I've got to talk with you."

"Yes, I know," she said, "but before that happens, there's something I'd like to have you do for me. Tomorrow, I want you to meet some friends of mine. I'd like you to get to know them a little, to learn what they do."

I was tired myself, and I guess I sounded like it when I asked her what kind of friends. "Will you trust me about this?" she asked. "It's really important. Can you meet Helena at the Net office about 11 a.m.?"

"Okay. Why not?" I said. "Then can you and I get together in the afternoon or at supper?"

"I hope so," she answered, and said good night.

*　　*　　*

The next morning, I got to the Net office well before the appointed time, thinking that I might run into her. No luck; a bearded man who was typing in the small reception room told me that Helena Tarazi expected me but was in a meeting. I sat down to wait and a few minutes later Yusuf showed up. He asked if I had any coffee, waved aside the bearded man's offer to get some with "Do it myself," and disappeared behind an inner doorway. He was back in seconds with cups for both of us.

"Helena tells me she'll be free in a moment and you can see the rest of the place," he said. "It really serves us very nicely. This building is owned by the family of someone in Net and we pay almost nothing for it. Three, no, four other people in Net live in the building as I do. Actually, the rooms we're in are the owners' apartment. They're living outside the country right now."

I nodded and he continued, "That reminds me, if the fighting gets worse, you may have to grab a flight out of here. How about

53

visas? Can you get into other countries or would you go home?"

I assured him that I was ready to go practically any place in the Middle East and he nodded. "Good. Let's find Helena."

He guided me through a room where a couple of young women were running duplicating equipment and down an angled hall past closed doors. We found Helena standing at the window of a tiny room that seemed to be walled with bookcases.

"Ah, good morning," she exclaimed. "Did you have a peaceful night?"

Yusuf left us. "Please sit down," Helena said, and briskly began to deliver a lecture. It was a pattern that was repeated throughout the day, varying only in subject matter and speaker. I got a short, warm welcome, endless infusions of orange drink, soda, and coffee, and then deluges of facts and commentary. If I'd had more experience with Middle Eastern ways, I would have been suspicious, but all I knew was that they were talking to me—at a time of difficult distraction—because Miriam had asked them to. So I listened as best I could, head spinning, until it was over. When I try to remember, all that comes are impressions of impassioned people and images drawn by quick-flowing words of Arabic-accented English:

Helena, tall, dark eyes alight: "Women in the Arab world are to help men and raise families. That is the situation where we find ourselves in Christian churches. So we honor tradition. But we look to the future. . . . We believe in the equality of all humans, women and men. . . . People like us in Net have a goal for women in the Arab countries. It is to share in the creation of a new society of faith, love and service. . . . Starting from the home, teaching Christ to our children, striving with men to create real Christian families, working in religious education and service in our churches. . . . But also (she leans toward me intensely) participating in government, in humanitarian organizations, in mass media, in artistic endeavor. . . . We are building up committees in our countries to seek these goals. . . . They will gather resources for women, they will study the realities of women's lives in our countries today, they will start church projects—summer camps for family life education, workshops on women's economic status in families, consultations on the role of women in Arab society, investigations of women's status under civic law. . . . Do you have any questions? No? Fine. Now I shall find Nabil for you."

She leaves and I look at the books surrounding me; their titles are in Arabic, English, French. I hear footsteps in the hall and turn to shake hands. Nabil is courtly and casual, mustachioed, a civil engineer. He is delighted to know that I have run a construction

54

company.

"I have my own consulting firm here in Beirut. But I spend as much time as I can as a volunteer in the churches' work for relief and rehabilitation. I myself am a refugee. When the war started, the Falangists asked me to join them in the fighting. I would not. So we lost everything we had. Our house was blown up. . . .

"What are the churches doing in relief and rehabilitation? A bit of everything. Top priority: rebuilding of schools—schools run by the churches—that were ruined in the fighting. . . . A quarter million people were displaced by the fighting in Southern Lebanon and we try to help them with temporary shelter, clothing, blankets, medicine, food. . . . Help comes to us from Christians all over the world. The World Council of Churches, Church World Service in your own country. . . . It is very welcome, but please, tell your friends to send only clothes and blankets that are clean. And the food, if it can be food that our people know, in portions that they can use. . . . And of course money, and freedom to use it in ways that will meet the greatest needs. . . . We need help. But the decision-making about that help—about all Christianity in the Arab countries—should be left to the Christians here. . . . What more can I tell you? We are trying to help people get back on their feet again. We would help them plant new orchards, almond groves, olive groves, even to turn again to producing natural silk. We get sandals and kitchen utensils for people. . . . We have so many projects to help people—a community center for the elderly, medical care for those suffering mental and nervous disorders from the war, financial help for widows to start small businesses, community centers, day-care centers, places where orphans or very poor children can be cared for. . . .

"Ah, well, so much to be done. But so good if the churches can plan together, can work together, cooperatively, don't you think? Ah, my friend, I can see that I have tired you. Let us see if Elias can come and visit with you. His interest is in youth work. Talking with him will make you young again!"

Elias looks like a soccer player, stocky, broad-shouldered. He gives me an easy grin, introduces himself as a Greek Orthodox layman, and then shrugs. "Why should I say that? Nabil and I are brothers in Christ, which is more important than my being Orthodox and his belonging to the National Evangelical Church. Right?" He shakes his head in self-disapproval and then claps his hands:

"Well, welcome! You are one of us, did you know that? We think of you as youth here. To be that means to be anywhere from fifteen to thirty-five years old, maybe more. It all depends on potential. If you want to be youth, you must be with potential to renew the churches, to renew society. You understand? (I'm not sure, but I let it go. Like the others, he is off and running. Why did Miriam set things up this way?) We do so many things, we try to do many things in our youth programs. You know—work camps, leadership training, exchange programs, study tours, publications. Not easy, of course, no, not easy. We have gone through suffering, tension, despair, conflict. And now (he waves toward the window) more fighting. Think how many problems this makes for youth. We have been trying to set up a work camp, international work camp, boys and girls from Europe, maybe North America, as well as here. But you cannot have something like that when there is fighting going on. . . .

"I will tell you what we try to do in our programs. One, we help youth with prayer, Bible study, participation in worship and liturgical life, we want them to grow as witnesses for Christ in the churches and in all of life. Two, help them grow toward one another, help them realize that they belong to the one church. This is the ecumenical idea and so important in a region like the Middle East to bring together people from different countries so that together they can witness and serve and seek peace and justice. We hope, too, to bring them into contact with the rest of the world and all of Christianity. That is three. . . .

"And, also, youth should be a time of learning. We want to help our young people learn to express their opinions in their own churches and communities. We want the youth movements in the different churches to learn to work together more. And Christian young people should be open to dialogue with other Christians and non-Christians, too, and they should learn how to act in such meetings. We want them to learn about their faith and so we try to have study seminars, following in the steps of the Apostle Paul by taking a tour to Turkey, for example. You see, we have lots going on. That's what it means to be young, right?—to have so much going on?"

Charles has lunch with me at a neighboring restaurant. He is a portly man of middle years, the vice-president of an advertising agency, who tells me that writing poetry is his avocation. His particular interest in the churches is radio broadcasting: "The air waves are our element. Using them, the churches reach people in many lands. . . . Ah, yes, we must be ecumenical indeed in our worship and evangelistic messages. There is so much to be covered—church history, Bible study, church news and the like. . . . But also we try to broadcast music and meditations, report youth activities, and provide commentary on family life. . . . Many radio listeners are the younger set, young people for whom music has an appeal that cannot be resisted. So we must do more music. . . . Church broadcasting here has been sternly tried in recent years. The war laid a heavy hand on us. Equipment lay idle, disintegrating for a year. Arrangements for reader reaction and for volunteer support were greatly harmed. We are recovering only gradually."

When we return to the Net office, Charles leads me to a large room where a dozen or so men and women are apparently at the end of a meeting. Miriam is present and I catch her quick smile of greeting as we enter. She looks at me with something of questioning or expectancy in her eyes. Helena, Nabil and Elias are there, too, but all the others are unknown to me, and in the flurry of introductions, I lose their names. We sit and relax a few minutes—more coffee again—and then the conversation picks up, gains speed, generates fervor. It sparks back and forth across the room, crackling with emotion:

". . . .No, we'll never have peace here until Israel settles as it should with the Palestinians, justly. . . ."

". . . . As far as I am concerned, the Syrians are a stabilizing force among us, but their massive shelling, falling on ordinary people, is very bad. But Syria looks after its own interests above all, naturally. We are on Israel's northern border and Syria is very interested in the kind of neighbor we'll be. . . ."

"Israel is too! That is why they help the Maronites. They tell the rest of the world they are helping the Christian Maronites survive but what they really want is to keep the Maronites in charge in Lebanon. They do not care that the Maronites should no longer run the country, that the majority of Lebanese probably don't want that. They just want the Maronites in charge of the government that is on their northern border."

"And so the Christians in Lebanon—I mean Maronites and Orthodox and Evangelical—are being pulled apart by outside influences when we need to be together. . . ."

". . . .When you say that, you must speak of Islam and the entire Middle East. There are only twelve or fourteen million Christians in the whole area. We are very much a minority. In the past we have been tolerated and sometimes even respected by Muslims. But now we face a dilemma. . . ."

"Yes! Very true. A serious situation. There is a revival in Islam. It may take an anti-Christian turn. With the great wealth of the Arab states, Islam considers that now is the time to put itself on the world map."

"You must understand how easy it is for people of the Middle East to see Christianity and the Western world as the same thing. And Western colonial powers have oppressed the Arab peoples, you know. Now Islam's rising power can be asserted against this oppression of the past."

"True, true, but we must explain to our friend from America that there is also fear of Christianity in Islam. In the West, state and religion are separate. Not so in Islamic tradition, where everything, government, politics, everything is part of religion. If Western influence—and all your technology and other things are very tantalizing—continues to increase, it threatens Islamic tradition."

"Yes, you have put it well. The ultra-conservative Muslim wants to confine Christians in a tight political structure, so they will not create that kind of atmosphere."

"How ironic it is that you find this same point of view in Israel. Some of its most powerful political leaders want state and religion to be locked together in the countries of the Middle East. That's the way it is in Israel. Do you know that Palestinians, those who would return to where they came from in what is now Israel, are, for all practical purposes, barred from citizenship but that a Jew from any country in the world can become an Israeli citizen almost immediately?"

"What these people—extreme conservatives, Muslim and Israeli—want in the Middle East is theocratic government. They fear the changes in their society that might occur if state and religion were separate, if governments were secular."

"Yet Lebanon's only hope is a secular government. We need to reform our system in a democratic way, particularly the election laws. Our old system, based on religion, no longer truly represents the people. We need to work together to create a new system that will give everyone an equal voice."

"Oh, yes! Yes! You see, Lebanon is the place where this is being fought out!"

The talking was interrupted increasingly at the end of the afternoon by departures and finally there was a common rising and leave-taking. I waited until Miriam finished talking with a couple of people.

"I kept my part of the deal," I reminded her.

"Okay, it's a date," she responded, laughing.

I called for her an hour later, at the apartment in the Net building where she and Helena were staying. She was wearing a white vest and slacks, a black satin blouse, and earrings, and she looked terrific.

I told her so after we had given our orders in the Maryland's dining room.

"Well, thank you," she said. "It's a sort of special occasion, isn't it?"

I nodded. "It's much pleasanter than I thought it would be. So pleasant that I wish I could forget why we're here. But I can't. Your father would like to have you come home."

Her eyes did not leave mine, and she said quietly, without hesitation, "If you were I, what would you do?"

I told her that I knew her parents were old, that I could understand how they felt, but that I couldn't answer her question. "I'm just beginning to know you," I said. So we talked about her for a while, about being a shy little girl, the only child of a strong-willed father and a mother who had a predilection for country clubs and dinner parties. A girl who liked to read and, doing so, became aware of flaws in her parents' values. Who developed standards of her own and friends of her own, who struggled to understand and accept her parents' love without letting it smother her. Who found strength to persevere in the discovery of her own identity with the aid of two or three friends—a woman professor in college whose enthusiasms were the women's movement and Russian literature, a boy she'd met in high school, a campus minister.

"Now I understand 'The Way of the Pilgrim,'" I commented.

"It meant a lot to me. It still does. I read it at a time when I was almost lost, and I found my way in it again. I thought if I could make the pilgrimage to the Holy Land, I would be blessed. So I came and I was. That's how I got to Turkey and Egypt, that's why I'm here."

"Why did you give it to me?"

"Oh." She leaned back against the leather seat. She smiled a little. "I wanted you to know about me, I guess. I didn't like misleading you. I was sorry for you. I thought that perhaps it would do for you what it did for me."

Sorry for me? Why would she be sorry for me?

She looked up and saw me watching her, did not turn away, and then asked, "What did you think of today, of the talks you had with people, of the people themselves?"

"What can I say? What great people. I admire them and what they're trying to do, more than I can say."

Her eyes held mine. "That's why I'm not going back with you, Amon. Can you understand?"

I was confused, then disappointed, then hurt and a little angry. "You mean you think they need you here? It's not safe, you know."

"It's my needing them, not their needing me."

"Your parents need you," I retorted.

She took the crack without flinching. She looked at her watch. "I've got to get back before dark," she reminded me.

She didn't want me to accompany her because daylight would be gone before I could return. I insisted, so she walked swiftly, saying very little.

At her doorway, I asked if perhaps the next day . . . .

"Amon, I'm sorry. I'm not going to be here tomorrow. I'm leaving for Jerusalem." She looked up the street, then at me, hesitated, and said, "Please hurry home. Be careful." The door closed behind her.

CHAPTER
FOUR

JERUSALEM, of course, meant that Miriam would be going to Israel, and Israel meant the special friend she had mentioned to me, "a boy I met in high school."

I was still suspicious after my talk with Yusuf the next morning. He had phoned me a little after six. Someone he knew had a ticket for a flight to Amman the next day but wouldn't be able to use it. Did I want it? "I guess so. I don't know. Let me think. I'll come over to see you."

Miriam was going to Jerusalem, Yusuf said, because the Assads and her friends at Net had persuaded her that the time was right to do it: Beirut wasn't safe, a church agency in Jerusalem was looking for someone to work with Palestinian refugees, she had long wanted to see the city. I made a skeptical remark about her knowing some man there and he responded with a puzzled look and then a shrug.

"May be," he said. "We thought you might go with her. She asked us to talk with you yesterday; she said she wanted you to know about our work. We thought it was in her mind that you might go along and spend a little time helping out with the refugee program.

But I guess things didn't work out?"

"You could say that," I answered dourly, and changed the subject to the trip to Amman. Yusuf was leaving on the first leg of a business trip to Kuwait; one of his associates had cancelled out so his ticket was available to me.

I spent the rest of the day with Yusuf who had to inspect a couple of reconstruction jobs. We got away late the next afternoon, after once again taking a detour away from the area of the fighting.

"I feel like I'm running out on friends," I told Yusuf as we took off.

"I know," he responded. "Let us hope for the best."

For an instant, I was back in Cairo, along the Nile with Kazuo Nakamura. "Somebody—a Japanese American preacher, if you can believe it—told me once, 'Live a life of hope,' " I said, and told him about Nakamura.

He nodded. "Good words for us right now. Do you ever read theology? I think your friend meant even more than I was saying. I mean, we hope for the safety of those we love. But we—and they, and everybody else, too, no matter who or what they are—have a greater hope than that. It is hope like faith. We believe that Jesus Christ has saved the world. He is victorious. So no matter what happens to us now, or our dear friends, we know that everything will finally, on the last day of the whole world, turn out all right."

I had never heard the thought put quite that way, and would have liked to discuss it a little. But Yusuf had something else to say:

"Yesterday afternoon, when we were talking about the problems of Christians being a minority, an important new idea was overlooked. That's human rights. You Americans are for human rights, and you're right. The principles on which human rights are based are Christian principles, so you're right. What I want to say is this: In the Middle East, perhaps Christians belong here on the basis of human rights. For a thousand years and more, we have lived here on the acceptance of Islam, not a comfortable way to exist. And we are not comfortable in Israel because most of us are Arabs as well as Christians, and the Israelis merely tolerate our presence as kind of second-class citizens. Now some of us are beginning to think that our existence should not be based on the tolerance of others but because we have the human right to exist."

"I see what you mean," I said. "Well, that might be one good thing we can do for you. We seem to have made plenty of problems for you."

He looked at me questioningly and I said, "For example, to most

Arabs—the vast majority of whom are Muslims—Christianity and America are the same thing. Arabs say that Israel is the 51st state of the United States, right? So, in their eyes, to be a Christian means to support Israel, a country despised by Arabs."

"Yes." He nodded. "For many Arabs that is true."

I shook my head. "I wish I could figure out an answer to the whole mess."

"Well, that's why Net works for reconciliation," he said. "When we help people, we don't ask what they are. We try to feed them, heal them, teach them, shelter them, whatever their religion or nationality. What better way to show that all of us are one?"

We arrived at the Amman airport at dark and got a cab into the city. Yusuf was staying overnight with a family he knew, but he helped me find a hotel on King Hussein Street before we parted. I hadn't decided what I was going to do, so he told me he'd get in touch with me the next day.

Amman was riding a building boom, acquiring business that had once gone to Beirut. My hotel was a rush job, jerry-built, yet fascinating in the way it contrasted new and old Arabia.

The room I got was a 12-foot cubicle, no air-conditioning, a sign in the bathroom about the city's shortage of water, windows wide open on an air shaft and facing other open windows that issued the cries of babies, the voices of adults, and the wailing beat of Arabic radio music. Within the big cubicle was a tiny one, a refrigerator gamely struggling to cool its cargo of soda, bottled water, beer, and liquor. Outside my room, down the hall, a door was open to another guest room. When I passed it, I looked in: a swarthy, fat, white-robed man lounged regally on the floor, selecting morsels of meat and fruit from a heaped platter while two servants squatted in attendance.

A few days before, I would have been disturbed by the strangeness, but now it intrigued me. I realized that my time in the Middle East was very short, that I must savor it at every opportunity. And so, in a paradox of logic that might have troubled my new Arab friends, I concluded that I could never hope to understand the Middle East without visiting Israel, without experiencing Jerusalem.

Instead of finding Yusuf in the lobby the next morning, I was confronted by a burly Arab businessman with a broad smile. He identified himself as Abu Said, come to bring me to his home, where Yusuf was staying. "Yusuf sick," he said with a lugubrious head shake.

Yusuf's affliction was similar to my ailment in Cairo. He was uncomfortable but functioning. When I told him I had decided to go to Jerusalem, he shook his head and said dryly, "I'm so surprised."

Jordanian law requires that anyone going from Amman to Israel stay in Jordan at least 48 hours. Abu Said helped me with arrangements and on my last evening in Amman, he brought me to his house to dine with his family and Yusuf. He and his wife had five children, ranging from an eighteen-year-old son studying science at the University of Amman to a dark-eyed, nine-year-old daughter who was one of the prettiest little girls I'd ever seen. They had lived in Jordan for only a couple of years, having spent the fifteen years before in Saudi Arabia, where Abu Said had worked as a surveyor. He'd saved enough money to invest in a partnership with a couple of friends in Amman—a plumbing and heating business.

They were a happy, intimate family. Yusuf told me that they were Muslims, and a picture of the Qur'an hung in the living room, above a book case that supported a tape deck.

As I left, we stood outside their stone house and looked across the road to ranks of similar houses ascending a wide, treeless hillside. Abu Said swept the scene with the wave of a hand and made a comment in Arabic. Yusuf translated for me: "All the people living there are Palestinians. There are more than a million of them in Jordan—over half the population—and other thousands living elsewhere in the Middle East, all displaced from their homeland as the result of the creation of Israel."

The next morning, I was up early and checked out of the hotel when Yusuf and Abu Said arrived. We picked up my papers at the Ministry of the Interior and raced back to the bus station, where Abu Ali negotiated a fair price for my limousine ride to the border. We shook hands and said goodbye. Just before the car pulled away, Yusuf stuck his head in the window. "By the way," he said, "remember Bir Zeit University. Bir Zeit. Miriam's supposed to be staying with a friend there." He gave me a big grin. "Say hello for me. I mean, if you see her."

A fast ride across barren, sun-blasted desert brought me to a reception area where Jordanian soldiers checked my papers and luggage. Lines of people were waiting under the corrugated iron roof. Gradually we were shepherded onto antique buses. When mine was full—I was standing in the aisle among old ladies and little kids, all sweating and seemingly befuddled as I was—we lurched off down a bumpy road.

Ten minutes later we stopped amid a clump of small, dusty trees. Someone who spoke a little English explained to me that the buses—three others were ahead of us—had to wait until the Israelis could check the passengers of those already across the border.

Twenty minutes later, we were still there, so I got out with some of the other passengers and walked around the bus to see what lay ahead. And there it was, the crack in the wall between the Arab world and Israel, the Allenby Bridge, a one-lane, planked span that looked to me like something a farmer back home might stretch across a big creek on his property. At each end were sand-bagged strong points where Jordanian and Israeli soldiers kept watch on one another.

Our time finally came. We rumbled over the planks and I caught a quick glimpse of the Jordan River, a muddy little stream banked by nondescript saplings.

An Israeli officer in fatigues—the universal uniform, I discovered, often bleached and mended from long wear—singled me out as a tourist and politely told me in English that I'd be taken to a special reception area. He seemed vigilant but cordial, reinforcing what I'd heard about the high quality of the Israeli army. At our next stop, however, I encountered a contrasting character who said he was a taxi driver from Chicago. He informed me he'd been born in Israel and returned every summer for forty-five days of service in the army. When he learned about the conditions I had witnessed in Lebanon, he shook his head and boasted, "We're going to have to go in there again." And when I asked if I could wait in the shade where my fellow passengers had gathered, he told me jauntily that it was okay if I could stand the smell.

The tourist baggage inspection was painstakingly thorough; everything I had was examined. It was also efficient and I found a Mercedes waiting outside to take me to Jerusalem.

The land across the Jordan was still flat and arid and oppressed by the same searing sun. At two Israeli checkpoints, the soldiers squinted at my papers from beneath the shade of wide-brimmed hats that lacked any trace of the military in their lineage.

After a half hour, we entered a fairly large town whose palm trees gave it an oasis-like quality. "Jericho," the driver told me as we wound around a town circle inscribed by souvenir shops. I couldn't help looking for the remains of the wall that had tumbled for Joshua.

Farther on, just before we started to climb a range of hills, the driver pointed to the left and told me that I was looking at the Dead Sea. It seemed a long way off, a long broad brush stroke of watery blue at the foot of bleached tan slopes.

I identified the ride's other major landmark myself. Shortly after we climbed from the valley floor, the high horizon ahead began to define the shapes of domes and towers. Leaning forward and pointing at them, I asked, "Jerusalem?" and the driver nodded.

At Abu Said's suggestion, I gave the driver the name of a hotel east of the old city, in a Palestinian village called Silwan. A relative of his was one of the owners. When I asked for him at the desk, the clerk left for a moment and came back with an open-faced man who introduced himself as Mohammed Salah, the manager and son of the man I asked for. His face lighted at Abu Said's name, we talked for a few minutes, and he had the clerk sign me in. When I walked into my room, I found myself facing a balcony with a sweeping view of the Garden of Gethsemane and the walls of the Old City.

After a shower, I went out on the balcony and, using a map I'd picked up at the border inspection building, figured out the landmarks that I could see. The hotel was apparently on the Mount of Olives and down below I could see trees in the Garden of Gethsemane and some church buildings. Jerusalem itself was close across the Kidron Valley, its Old City enclosed in immense stone walls that made it look like a giant old fortress clinging to the hillside. I could identify only one building: the glinting gold bowl of the mosque known as the Dome of the Rock.

The place names had been familiar to me since Sunday School, yet I had difficulty making a connection between what my eyes saw and what my memory recalled of the earth-shaking wonder and mystery somehow evoked in a small boy in a little backwoods church.

Sacrilegious? Not really. I'd come to Jerusalem because almost everything I'd learned about the Middle East seemed to tie in, somehow, with Jerusalem or Israel—politics, religion, war, whatever. I'd been caught up in people's lives and problems, but there was something missing in what I knew or understood, and I wanted to find it.

Thinking that way brought me to Miriam. Of course, at the time, on the balcony, looking out on Jerusalem, I simply started thinking of her. I didn't realize the inevitability of it until later. Then, I began to wonder where out there she might be, what she might be doing. After all, now that I was in Jerusalem, I really should make an effort to talk with her again. Her father and mother would expect me to. And perhaps we should, for our own sakes. We were friends and it would not be right for friendship to break off with the abruptness of our parting in Beirut. Even if she would not come home, perhaps she would want to give me some message for her family.

This line of reasoning seemed very persuasive and I decided to start out looking for her the next morning. In unexpectedly good spirits, I went to dinner. The hotel dining room was on the top floor and provided a lofty view of Jerusalem. By the time I arrived, it was almost filled with church people from Denmark who were touring the Holy Land. I shared a table briefly with a Danish matron and her towering adult son. After they left, the hotel manager came over to greet me and, as we talked, one of his brothers, Mahmoud, joined us. At my insistence, they sat down and a waiter brought them coffee.

I confessed that I was less interested in Jerusalem as a tourist site than as a place of importance in the modern Middle East. "For example," I said, "I'd like to know what it feels like to live in Jerusalem or in Israel today."

Mahmoud, who was younger and more excitable than Mohammed, wagged a finger at me. "Please. Despite what the Israelis say, this is not Israel. This is Palestine. I will tell you how it feels to be a Palestinian. How would you like it if you had a house and someone said, here is a man who has no place to live, let him stay in one of your rooms? So he comes to live in the room and what happens? Pretty soon he takes over the whole house and wants to kick you out. That is how Palestinians feel about Israel."

"You see, Mr. Smith," Mohammed said more calmly. "We do not feel that Americans understand what it is like in the Middle East. They think of oil. They think of how Israel is necessary because of everything that happened to Jews in World War II. But do they think that there are three and a half million Palestinians in the world and only 500,000 are citizens of Israel?"

"Yes. Abu Said told me something about that."

Mahmoud kept his finger under control but his passion for discussion had not abated. "Is it not true that U.S. papers give the impression that Palestinians are all terrorists and that the Palestine Liberation Organization is always killing, always blowing up? Do you know what Palestinians who can no longer live here are doing in the Middle East? More Palestinians can read and write, more have college degrees than any other Arabs anywhere. Who runs most of the businesses in Jordan? Palestinians like Abu Said. Who helps the Syrians keep their government operating? Palestinians. Who publishes more newspapers and magazines for Arabs than Palestinians? Nobody. And Palestinian working men do the labor that is needed in all those places and in Israel, too."

"Well, I think people at home are beginning to understand some of what you say," I said, trying not to sound too defensive. "Some of us know that the PLO isn't all violent. We know that it's made up of a number of groups that don't always agree about terrorism."

"That is good," Mohammed told me, nodding. "Right now, here on the West Bank, Palestinians support the PLO. It's really the only organization they have to represent them in the politics and struggle for power in the area."

"I'm confused about the West Bank," I said. "On the map, it looks like a big chunk of land between the Jordan River and Jerusalem, but I haven't seen any signs or boundary markers."

The brothers laughed and Mahmoud touched my arm. "You are here," he said. "This is the West Bank. When you came across the bridge you came into it, and all the way here, you were in it. It's land just like other land. It used to be in Jordan, but since the '67 war, the Israelis have controlled it. It's really our land and they should give it back to us. Even the United Nations says they should give it back."

"To you Americans, it seems very savage that Palestinian terrorists assassinate men or set bombs to blow people up," Mohammed told me. "It is cruel and unjust, you say, to kill innocent men and women. But you must realize the injustice and cruelty of the Israelis in taking our land, depriving Palestinians of their homes, taking away our source of food, bringing death to our people. They are still doing this, building new settlements on land that is not theirs. Are Palestinians not to fight against this? If you say that the Israelis do not murder as terrorists do, what do you call their bombing and strafing of refugee camps?"

"I know such injustice myself," Mahmoud said. "The Israelis threw me in jail and beat me up. The reason: because a bomb went off in a section of Jerusalem where I happened to be and they picked up all the Palestinian men around there. I had done nothing, but they beat me up. And other people, too."

Mohammed pointed out the window toward the west, as if to indicate the part of Jerusalem where the Israelis live. "They are like foreigners among us," he said. "They were put here. They are smart and they are strong. But they will lose, finally. We will overcome if it takes a hundred years. You remember that the Crusaders ruled Palestine at one time. But finally we overcame them."

I understood and even sympathized with the two men, but I couldn't help thinking that, had I been with Israelis, I would have heard completely opposite accusations, just as impassioned, just as persuasive.

"Isn't there any solution?" I asked. "What about a Palestinian homeland in the West Bank and the Gaza Strip? Wouldn't that work?"

Mohammed shrugged. "Will the Israelis agree to that? Let them agree and then we shall see."

"Meanwhile, we are supposed to wait and do nothing?" Mahmoud demanded. "Refugees are suffering, they eat crumbs, they live in rotting tents. . . . "

When we got up to leave, I asked them about my getting to Bir Zeit University. "While I'm in Jerusalem, I'd like to see a friend of mine who's there."

Rather than give me directions, they decided that Mahmoud would drive me to the university the next morning. What a mercurial pair—filled with bitterness and anger one moment, considerate and hospitable the next.

I was dead tired after a full day, and eager to get to bed, but when I got to my room, the view of Jerusalem at night drew me to the balcony. Across the valley, the city lay in a jewelry of lights, couched for the night among hills that reached for the stars. Floodlighting transformed its old walls to pale amber cliffs. An orange crescent moon hovered over a silhouetted tower and as I stood, entranced by the beauty, I could almost see its descent toward the horizon.

Standing there, I realized I wanted Miriam to be my wife. I can't remember or explain how it happened. I suppose I thought again of her being somewhere in the city that lay before me. And I may have wondered why I was so troubled by her refusal to come back to the States. I know I felt very much alone. I guess I discovered the emptiness of my life and knew that, if I were walking in Jerusalem at that moment and met her, I would be filled with joy.

It could never be. Impossible! And yet its impossibility made it irresistible; it was a discovery that could not be achieved but had to be tried. The reaching gave beauty and meaning to what could not be reached.

*   *   *

The next morning, when Mahmoud drove me north to Bir Zeit, I was delighted with the beauty of the countryside. The road zig-zagged through rolling, flower-filled grazing land and I remarked that the countryside was the first I'd seen that matched biblical descriptions of a land flowing with milk and honey.

Mahmoud was surprised by my enthusiasm, but he agreed with me. "Yes, and there is farmland much more fertile than this. It has always been so, even though the Israelis will tell you that they are the ones who made it that way."

Bir Zeit's campus was a modest one, a kind of village among the hills, all of whose occupants seemed to have long hair, blue jeans, and armloads of books. Mahmoud was puzzled by my lack of an address for Miriam or her friend, but he willingly acted as my interpreter as we moved from one office to another. People were patient and tried to be helpful but their answer was unanimous: there was no one around, visitor or otherwise, known as Miriam Assad or even Mary Salter.

On the way home, to cheer me up, he said he was sure I would find her eventually. When I told him that the only possibility was to contact the church refugee office, he exclaimed, "Hey, you are in luck. Tonight, at the hotel, there will be a Christian man who is a member of that organization. He is Mr. Zakouris, who owns the gift shop in our hotel. He comes every week this night to talk with his manager in our hotel."

I didn't see how Mr. Zakouris could be much help to me, but I told Mahmoud I'd be grateful for an introduction. Before we returned to the hotel, we stopped at a newsstand so I could buy a copy of *The Jerusalem Post* and learn about news from Lebanon. Mahmoud frowned at my choice of reading matter, but I went through it carefully when I was back in my room. Fighting was continuing in Beirut; it made the main story on the front page. A special section of the paper was titled "Girls and the Army." Apparently there was strong opposition by some Orthodox Jewish groups to conscription, or any form of army service, for women. One article told of four high school girls who were opposed to exempting women from military service on religious grounds. The article and their pictures indicated that they were intelligent and attractive people. Their parents' backgrounds reflected the variations in Israeli society: three of them were born in what is now Israel, one in Czechoslovakia, another in Poland, another in Iraq; one father had been born in Germany and had spent the years of World War II as a boy hiding in Holland, a mother was a survivor of concentration camps in Europe.

So even Israel, which from the outside world seemed to be made of one unified people, was really as much a mosaic of different elements as any other group or society in the Middle East: the Arab nations, the sects of Islam, the churches of Christianity. Perhaps diversity could be found everywhere in the world, but it seemed to me that nothing could match the contrasting differences in the Middle East.

The paper's advertisements told me something else: Jerusalem is in many ways a Western city, almost as much as Beirut. Its people buy dishwashers, use hearing aids, waste time watching silly TV programs, patronize drug stores that sell everything from pharmaceuticals to French pastry, and eat in Chinese restaurants.

70

There was one ad, however, that put all Israeli normality in ominous perspective: a simple statement that said, "Everything in its place. Report suspicious objects!"

A thunderous clap rattled my windows, startling me even though I knew it came from Israeli jets breaking the sound barrier as they made a pass high over the city. I dropped the paper and, rather than picking it up, lay back on my bed and stared at the ceiling.

What would I say to her? Best to be honest. Say what you feel. Say you love her. But can you say that? Does it make sense when you've only known one another a few days? Maybe not, but since when does love make sense? I cannot explain how I feel, I just feel that way. I love her enough to be her husband. I think I do. I would like to be her husband. I know that. I have been living in the dark. Have you ever been in the dark for a long time, and then the lights go on? That's what it was like when I realized that I loved her.

I had expected to find Mr. Zakouris a business type in tie and suit-coat, but he turned out to be a barrel-chested man in sport clothes, his tanned face contrasting with a white moustache and sharp blue eyes. He was courteous in a detached way until he learned of my associations in Beirut. "Say no more, Mr. Smith," he told me. "I would consider it a privilege to take you to the refugee committee offices tomorrow. We can make the inquiries that are necessary and I shall be of whatever additional service you may require."

The next day he picked me up at the hotel promptly at 9 a.m. and half an hour later had me at the refugee office. I could tell from the deference shown him by the staff that he was a person of importance. Unfortunately, his prominence couldn't solve the problem that confronted us there. People in the office knew that Miriam had been in touch with the executive director, Mr. Freija, but they didn't know what she had said and Mr. Freija himself was on a trip and wouldn't return until the next afternoon.

"So we shall leave word for Mr. Freija to call you as soon as he returns," Zakouris said. "Is there anything else we can do to find this young lady?"

"I don't know," I told him. "She could be almost anyplace. She's wanted to come to Jerusalem for a long time, she considers herself a pilgrim in a way, so I suppose she could be anywhere that pilgrims—Russian pilgrims, maybe—go."

"Very well, then," he replied. "I shall take you on a pilgrim's tour of Jerusalem. You should see my native city anyway. I have lived here all my life and I am a student of the church and of archeology. What do you say?"

Impatient and frustrated as I was, I agreed. I wanted to see Jerusalem's sites sometime and if we found Miriam, so much the better.

We started in the Kidron Valley east of the Old City and then went to the Garden of Gethsemane. The sun burned in a clear blue sky, tracing the old olive trees in sharp detail and accenting the lines and colors on the shrines and churches on the hillside. One of the buildings was the Russian Church of Mary Magdalene, Mr. Zakouris pointed out, so we took pains to inspect it. A number of other tourists strolled around us, but no Miriam. We had the same luck at a Russian chapel in the Garden.

When we returned to his car, I confessed that I had difficulty concentrating on the significance of the sites.

"Oh, that is quite understandable under the circumstances," he responded. "There will be other times when you can return, perhaps the two of you together.

"We are now ready," he continued, "to explore the Old City. There are eight gates," he instructed me, "and the Citadel and David's Tower. Part of the foundation of the Citadel is more than 2,000 years old. You can still see stones and tiles bearing the stamp of Roman legions that manned the fortress."

He parked at the Damascus Gate and guided me through the crowd clustered beneath its arch. Within the walls, we followed a route that seemed to have been burrowed out of rock: blocks of stone underfoot, shops like caverns stocked with multitudes of treasures, bouldered ceiling closing over us. People crowded about. Tourists wearing shorts, sunglasses, cameras, crazy hats, and with bargain-hunting eyes. Shopkeepers, beckoning us into their shops to see carpets, jewelry, fruit, silver, leather, candy, robes: "Welcome, it costs nothing to look, will you have tea as my guest?" A few clergy; I saw a priest standing in front of a tablet whose inscription began with a large Roman numeral IV.

I turned to Zakouris and started to ask, "Is that a station of the . . .?"

"Yes, of the Cross. See, this is the Via Dolorosa."

I looked up the old alley, at the people picking their way up and down its steps. What a long, hard climb for a man bearing a cross's timber. Then we reached a widening, a stone courtyard, a looming wall with a great door.

"This is the Church of the Holy Sepulcher," my companion said. "Shall we go in?"

I moved forward with him and then stopped. "The place where

Jesus is supposed to have been buried?" He nodded.

"Can we wait outside here and watch who goes in and comes out? I don't think I want to go in there just to look for someone."

We moved on after a while, had a leisurely lunch, and continued our exploration. By the afternoon's end, we had seen the four sections of the Old City—the Armenian, Christian, Jewish, and Muslim quarters. Churches, mosques, and synagogues beyond number. The Western Wall and the Dome of the Rock, so called because it encloses the rock from which Muslims believe Mohammed rode to heaven on his horse.

When Zakouris brought me back to the hotel, I insisted that he have coffee as my guest. Before we parted, I told him again how much I appreciated his help.

"Ah, Mr. Smith, I love this city," he said, "and take pride in showing it." But he spoke so soberly that I felt compelled to ask, after a moment, if perhaps something seen in our tour was troubling him.

"What gives me joy saddens me too," he answered. "We are losing Jerusalem, we Christians. It is our spiritual home, our birthplace, but it is slipping away from us. The Christian population is declining, the churches are losing their members. Consider my own family. I am my father's only survivor and I cling to the heritage he has given me in this city, in our church. But my son and my daughter had to go to Europe and the United States for their university work. They married persons from those places and there is where they live today. It is the same with most of our young people. Obtaining a higher education here is difficult for them. Even when they want to return from overseas, they are frustrated by the lack of housing. And so the churches here lose their members and grow weak. Is that not tragic? Should not the church be strong in Jerusalem, of all places in the world?"

The answer was obvious, so I asked, "Can't you do something about the problem? There are all kinds of churches here; can't they get together and build more universities and do something about financing housing?"

He looked at me fiercely. "We have a leadership problem. That is my answer to your question. Not everyone will tell you the truth, but some of the leadership of our churches is faulty. There are priests who are insensitive to the needs of the people. Why should the highest clergy in my church, for example, be Greek rather than Arab, like the people of the church? Why are the village priests so often poorly educated, so lacking in the ability to minister to the needs of the villages? And that is not the worst of the matter. The leadership in some of the religious groups is infected by corruption. They are rascals and I have told them to their faces."

I asked if the lay people of the churches, people like himself, could not bring some reformation.

"We have tried," he told me, "but it is very difficult. The clergy hold the power. And in these days when life is so uncertain, so difficult for many of our people, we are preoccupied with surviving as human beings. If a time of peace ever comes again, we shall be able to do what is needed."

"I think it would be very hard for you to worship in your churches when you often do not respect the clergy," I said.

He nodded and said slowly, "It is. All that we can do is tell ourselves that we must practice what they preach, not what they do. You can see how important our liturgy is to us in such circumstances. The liturgy is not corrupted."

"What do the Jews and Muslims think of all this?"

He shook his head. "I don't know. They have problems of their own. Besides, you should not ask an Arab what a Jew thinks. Ask a Jew."

"I would like to," I said, "but somehow I haven't come in contact with Israelis long enough for more than a few words. Hearing so much criticism of Israel makes me think I should get the other side. Does it bother you, as an Arab, to have me say that?"

"Not particularly. In fact, I have business associations with Israelis and can arrange for you to talk with some. I think of one man in particular, a lawyer—a former judge. How about tomorrow morning, before our friend Freija returns from the refugee camps?"

We agreed, and at 11 a.m. the next day I entered a handsome office building and was directed to a suite of offices on the first floor. Mr. Rosen came out of his office to greet me—a man who indeed looked like a judge— heavy-set, erect, white-haired.

He nodded politely as I explained my desire to talk to an Israeli after hearing so much of the Arab viewpoint. "I am only one person, of course, Mr. Smith, but I am sure that I speak for all Israelis in saying that we seek nothing but peace and prosperity for our neighbors as well as ourselves."

It seemed such a bland remark, in contrast with the criticism I had heard, that I wondered if he was giving me a line. So I told him bluntly about meeting the Israeli soldier who had boasted about invading Lebanon and had made the comment about my Arab companions on the bus.

He leaned forward, face flushed. "Most unfortunate. Intem-

74

perate, a childish remark that can be only understood by someone who knows how much the Jews have suffered. We have suffered at the hands of many peoples and I am afraid that some of us bear the scars, in one way or another."

He was a very interesting man, born in Palestine, and had been a soldier in the British army before the creation of Israel. As I listened to him, I was reminded of some of my Arab friends, for he seemed as committed and as inflexible a partisan of his nation as they were of theirs. He was as convincing, too, answering my questions with such complexity that I could remember only fragments:

"Israel is part of Judaism. We are commanded to rebuild Israel and Jerusalem must be part of Israel. . . . We have won the land, and when you have the land, you must not give it away. . . . Look at the nation we have created. There is more freedom in Israel than has ever existed before in this part of the world. Look at the holy places. We have made them open to all. It was not so before the '67 war, when the Arabs would not permit Jews to go to their holy places in the Old City. Before, when Jerusalem was conquered by the Crusaders or the Turks, it was terribly damaged. Compare with that the Israeli army, which was careful to protect the Christian holy places. . . . Tell me, in our wars with the Arabs, have you ever heard that our soldiers have been accused of rape? . . . . Have you seen our bountiful countryside, the fields, the orchards, the crops that are growing there now? . . . . I know that in some countries there is much talk about the Palestinian refugees. Sometimes I think that such concern is all out of proportion. There are displaced persons in other parts of the world, too, you know—Biafrans, Pakistani. Do you know how many Jews have been displaced? The village where I grew up was Jewish, but now it is an Arab town. . . . When you speak of refugees, you must realize that after the '48 war, nearly 800,000 Jews from Arab countries left the lands of their birth. They lost their property; they were refugees, and many of them found a home in Israel. Today, they and their children make up nearly 60 percent of Israel's Jewish population. . . . If the rest of the world would simply leave us alone, we could work out our problems. We must get to the point where we can forget what happened before and sit down together and talk. Once we begin to talk without cannons firing, we shall have peace. I think peace is coming, coming tomorrow. If our friends, if people of good will can only help us reach the negotiating table. . . . The Soviet Union is the big problem. . . . But peace is what we want. Look, when I was a young man I was willing to fight for Israel. I thought, if I fight now, my children can live in peace. But now I have a son and he is in the

75

army, too. That is not what I intended."

Our conversation didn't end until past noon, and Rosen invited me to lunch. I accepted but then changed my mind, thinking that I should get to the refugee office as soon as I could in the event that Mr. Freija had returned early. If that were so, perhaps I could get Miriam's address from him immediately and find her by the end of the day. The thought leveled everything else to inconsequence.

But Freija's office had bad news for me: "Sorry, sir, but he has been delayed and will not be returning as expected. He sent word just now by one of his helpers."

"Well, when will he be here?"

"I'm sorry, but we do not know."

My feelings must have shown, because the clerk excused himself and returned quickly, accompanied by a small, dark man in work clothes. "This man brought the message. You would like to ask him something?"

"When did he see Mr. Freija? Where is he? Can I get to him?"

Ah, that was possible! The two men talked in Arabic and the clerk translated: "If you wish to hire a car, Mr. Freija is at an old refugee camp, on the other side of Jericho. Maybe forty-five minutes away, on the road to the Allenby Bridge."

I had a faint recollection of seeing a refugee camp on my trip from Jordan to Jerusalem and I recognized the place shortly after my cab passed through Jericho. It stretched for half a mile along the highway, a barren expanse of yellow-white cinder block shacks with black, empty windows.

The driver and I found Freija talking with a couple of men in a one-room structure that carried a few hints—a broken chalkboard, a couple of desks—that it had once been used as a school. They permitted me to interrupt and I told Freija the purpose of my visit.

He listened attentively, a tall, brooding man with a soft voice.

"Yes," he said, "I have Miriam's address back at my office. It's in my files; she wrote it down for me when I was busy and I put it away without looking at it. So I'll have to dig it out for you."

"Can someone there get it for me?" I asked. "I know you don't expect to get back today."

"Well, we"—he gestured at the men with him—"are waiting for someone else to join us. As soon as he arrives, we can talk and then I'll be free. So I can go back with you. Indeed, I'll be glad to."

He returned to his conversation with the men and I went outside to tell my driver that we would wait for an hour or two. He nodded agreeably and we found a little shade and talked a while. I found that he, himself, was a refugee and had lived as a child in another refugee camp.

"After the '48 war, seven hundred fifty thousand Palestinians were refugees," he told me. "Now the number is much bigger, millions living in Jordan, Lebanon, Syria, Saudi Arabia, Kuwait and other places."

I nodded, waiting to hear more of his experiences. Instead, he motioned toward the lofty hills looking down on us from the north. "Important place for Christians," he said. "Mount of Temptation."

Yes, in flat country like this, it could be called a mountain. Its barren, dark slope was grim and austere, a lonely place from which a man might be tempted to flee to ease and softness and pleasure.

Freija's two companions left the abandoned schoolroom and he came to the doorway and beckoned me inside.

"They have gone to get the man we need to see," he explained. "Perhaps you will not have to wait so long."

He produced some tea from a curtained corner and listened to my report of my travels. As soon as I could, I turned the conversation back to his work with refugees.

"Your driver is one of about 300,000 refugees living in the West Bank," he said. "They make up almost half of its entire Arab population. Many of the refugees are like him: they've found work and new homes. But something like 100,000 refugees still live in camps like this one."

"That's a lot of people," I remarked. "How do they get by?"

"The main burden of feeding, sheltering and educating is carried by the United Nations Relief and Works Agency. I've heard figures that it costs UNRWA about ten cents a day per refugee—seven cents for food and medicine, three cents for education and training. These people are very poor, of course. They are very bitter about it, too. They have received no money for the homes they were forced to leave."

"Your office is connected with churches, not UNRWA, right?"

"Yes, for, of course, the refugees need all the assistance they can get. We work with West Bank refugees. Our efforts now emphasize three things: health education, employment opportunities, and community development. Miriam and I will have to talk about what she will do. Right now, because the work doesn't have enough money to do everything that is needed, we are concentrating on sixteen or seventeen villages that are most desperate for help. Some need roads, some need clinics or water systems or schools, some need more than one thing. Lack of decent school facilities is a common problem;

77

school children frequently suffer because their classrooms lack good light or ventilation. Some have to go to other villages for school, a difficult thing in bad winter weather, so they stop attending and they fall behind and never catch up on the education they need today."

"Even those activities must cost a lot of money," I said.

"Oh, yes, but the village people themselves help out. They give money, too, and land, building materials, their own labor, never less than half of the project's cost and sometimes as much as eighty percent. This is hard for them to do, for they are mostly farmers and their land is not very good. But they are wonderful people. The spirit of self-help is catching fire. They have strong faith in God. This brings them hope. And when they know that our committee's money comes from the church people of other nations who care for them, this increases their hope."

"You must find much satisfaction in such work."

"Yes, but so much more could be done. You have not been to the Gaza Strip, south of here, have you? There are about 240,000 other refugees in camps there, fed and sheltered with UN funds. Many of the young people among the refugees work as laborers but they cannot earn enough to support their families. One thing our churches try to do there is to provide vocational training for boys and girls so they can find better jobs. They come to our training centers, spend a couple of years, learn a trade, set up their own shops. The girls, for example, learn dressmaking, secretarial skills, and knitting. Sometimes, we are able to give scholarships to universities. In addition to education, we provide family centers and medical assistance such as artificial limbs and braces for children who are crippled by polio."

"Miriam probably would be interested in any of the things you've mentioned. I know she worked with families of garbage collectors in Cairo," I said. Then a second thought came to me, quite unbidden: "If I were any good at that sort of thing, I think I might like to help, too."

Perhaps, if we had talked long enough, he would have mentioned something in the construction line that might really have interested me. We were interrupted, however, by the return of the men he'd been talking to, in company with the one they wanted. I excused myself and brought a cup of tea out to my driver.

On the way back to Jerusalem, Freija told me that he had been discussing the situation in the camp with the three men. They were concerned about their families and he was explaining the work of an organization called the Family Revival Society. I asked if he would tell me about it.

He nodded his appreciation. "Family life is very important. Here on the West Bank this society works for people whether they are Christians or Muslims. In particular, it tries to help women of all ages and all social classes. It wants to raise the standard of women, culturally, financially, socially. It tries to help the poor. And also to preserve and develop Palestinian handicrafts. It helps girls find occupations. It assists working women by providing a day-care center and a kindergarten for their children. You will understand that education is very important for refugee children. It will help them have dignity despite the poverty in which many of them must live. The society helps them to see that they are the future generation that is going to be free and to live in happiness and dignity.

"If we had more time, we could visit the society, in a town called Bireh. But maybe later you can see something similar that the YWCA is doing with educational and vocational programs for young girls in Jerusalem and some surrounding towns."

"Really? I didn't realize that such work went on in Jerusalem. I suppose I have the typical tourist impression that church activities there are pretty much things connected with shrines and things."

"Oh, no. There is more. Something else that might interest you is the Quaker Service office, not too far from Herod's Gate. It provides legal aid and community information service, both of which are important for Palestinians who don't understand their rights under Israeli law."

The refugee office was closed when we got there, but Freija let us in with his key. As soon as we entered his office, he opened a file drawer and extracted an ordinary envelope. "Ah, here it is." He pulled a slip of paper from it. He seemed about to read it aloud as his eyes scanned it, but instead he was silent, studying it. Finally, he looked at me and with a slight, quizzical tilt of his head, said, "Seaview Manor, Netanya."

"What's that?" I asked. "Very far?"

"No. No. Probably a couple of hours north of here on the coast. But I'm a little surprised."

"Why is that?"

"Netanya is probably a one hundred per cent Israeli community. I wonder why Miriam would be up there."

The words seemed to stick in my mouth, but I finally got them out: "She met an Israeli man back in the States a few years ago. She's probably up there to see him."

* * *

79

Netanya was a vibrant town, its downtown streets busy with small cars and lunch-hour crowds dining in outdoor restaurants.

"This is it," the driver of my rented limousine said and I paid him off. Seaview Manor confronted me from behind a wall of palm trees. It was a modern, ten-story block of blazing white cement, glass, and aluminum.

A couple of men were at the front desk and I asked one if they had a guest named Miriam Assad. He consulted the register and said, "I'm sorry, sir, we don't."

"Try Mary Salter."

He looked again and shook his head. "Sir, I'm. . . ."

The other man interrupted him, and they talked a moment in Hebrew before the clerk continued: "An American young woman?"

I nodded. "Yes."

He conferred with his colleague and turned to me. "She is not a registered visitor. I believe she may be a private guest of the management, but she is not here at present."

"Do you have any idea where I can find her? I've come all the way up here from Jerusalem."

"I see." He was businesslike, but I thought I saw a bit of camaraderie in his expression. "We don't provide information about our guests without their permission. She may return in a while. If you want to, you might take a walk down to the beach and then come back. Of course, she might be down there herself. . . ."

I got the idea. "Thanks, friend," I said.

I hadn't slept much the night before and the sun hit me like a sledge hammer when I walked across the patio to the steps down to the Mediterranean. A big stone refreshment stand beckoned me to its shade and I felt better after a couple of hot dogs and a soda. My plan was simple. I was going to find her and say what I had to say. If her friend was with her, so be it. I'd gone over everything in my head a hundred times: "I'm sorry to show up this way, Miriam, and you, too, whatever your name is, but Miriam, I have to tell you that I love you and want to ask you to marry me." That should get the subject on the table.

I plodded out through the sand again, feeling like a fool in all my clothes among those bathing suits and tanned bodies. I unbuttoned my shirt when I got to the wet, took off my shoes and socks, and rolled up my trousers. Then I started walking and looking. Without realizing it, I think I slowed down and squinted every time I saw a young woman and a man wading out of the surf or spied some couple close together under a beach umbrella. The day and the water were beautiful and a lot of people were having fun, but not me.

Well, I found her under an umbrella. It was a big umbrella, sheltering Mr. and Mrs. Ephraim Wolinski, their three small daughters—Efrat, Tali, and Leah—Mrs. Wolinski's parents, Mr. and Mrs. Barzilai, and Miriam.

I walked over and when she looked up, I said, "I'm sorry to show up this. . . ."

"Amon!" she cried. "Amon Smith! Ephraim, this is my friend, Amon Smith."

So much for the marriage proposal that day. I didn't lose my purpose entirely, but its urgency diminished radically when I grasped Ephraim's identity. He was the Jewish friend of her high school years, a nice, average kind of guy, undoubtedly successful as manager of Seaview Manor and unmistakably a husband, father, and son-in-law.

We spent the afternoon getting acquainted, reminiscing about Clarksburg, and taking Efrat, Tali, and Leah for a long and very splashy stroll along the beach. Only once were Miriam and I alone, when we retraced a few steps to pick up a sand pail that had been dropped.

"I like the way you look in that bathing suit," I said, a considerable understatement.

She ignored it. "Amon, why did you follow me? You know how I feel. I'm not ready to go home yet."

"You're not angry, though, are you? You're glad to see me, I can tell. You were glad to see me in Sidon, too. Do you realize how important that is?"

"No, I don't. You're not making sense."

I walked more slowly, trying to delay our catching up with the others.

"I'd like to talk with you some more," I said. "That's why I came here after you. I thought you and Ephraim had something going. I didn't know he was married and all that. I wanted to get here before. . . ."

She stopped and faced me, and I thought that we were going to say what needed to be said right there. But one of the little girls had come running back toward us and she stumbled and fell, just at that moment, sending up a wail of complaint. When we picked her up, she would not be comforted, so we hurried her back to her father's arms.

I hoped that Miriam might go back to Jerusalem with me that evening but the Wolinskis expected her to stay another night and she made no effort to shorten her visit.

"At least you can have dinner with us before you go, Amon,"

81

Ephraim said jovially. "The children will go to bed and we can have a little peace and quiet."

And that's what happened, surprisingly so, in view of the subject that held our attention. Mr. and Mrs. Barzilai went to bed shortly after their grandchildren, leaving Miriam, Ephraim, his wife, Claire, and me alone on the tiny terrace of the Wolinskis' apartment. Without conscious effort, we found ourselves talking about the future of Israel, Miriam and I speaking out of sympathy for Arab friends and Ephraim and Claire responding from their commitment to their country.

You see, Ephraim and Claire told us, it has become clear to Jews in this century that they and their children would never be able to live their own lives without their own country. The Holocaust in Europe taught them that. It created so many Jewish refugees that a state was needed to accommodate them. When the Jewish refugees came to Palestine, much of the land was not being used. The Palestinians did not have to leave; if they had stayed, they would be enjoying all the benefits of Western technology that Israel has introduced. They would have all been living in the kind of democratic state that exists no place else in the Middle East. The Palestinians who left their homes forfeited their right to land in Israel. They are refugees by their own choosing. Arab countries should take care of them as Israel is taking care of Jewish refugees. Today, if all the Palestinians were to return to Israel, Jews would be a minority in their own country.

Miriam was much better than I in responding. She said that she believed that the Jews had no stronger biblical or historical claim to Palestine than the Arabs. Sixty years ago or so, ninety per cent of the population of Palestine was Arab and only ten per cent was Jewish. From the Arab point of view, Israel is a state created by the West, by the United Nations and primarily with U.S. support. The Arab countries hate Western colonialism and see Israel as a tool of that colonialism. Jews have been given Arab land because Western Christians feel guilty about what happened to Jews in Europe before and during World War II. Arabs have been a persecuted people, too; what right did the United Nations have to take Arab land and give it to the Jews? As for Palestinians staying in Israel, they could not because of the war. The Israelis wanted them out to make more room for Jewish refugees. Speaking of the UN, why doesn't Israel do what the UN says and let the Palestinians back to their land, or at least pay them for it? It seems clear that Israel wants to grow in size at the expense of Palestinians.

No, Miriam, that is not true, her friends protested. Thousands of

Palestinian Arabs stayed after the '48 war. Today, more than 10 per cent of Israel's population is Arab. As for terrorists in neighboring countries—if those countries shield them, they will lose land. Arab countries do not realize how important it is for Jews to protect their holy places and their land. When the Arabs controlled East Jerusalem, they would not allow Jews to come to the holiest Jewish places. Jerusalem is the only holy city of the Jews; for Muslims, Mecca and Medina are equally if not more holy than Jerusalem. Arabs do not realize how important Israel is to Jews, Jews not only in Israel but everywhere in the world. Jews have suffered persecution everywhere but in Israel. There is the possibility that they may suffer again, but if they do, they can go to Israel. It is their lifeboat, their only lifeboat.

But Miriam and I made the point that we have heard so many times: Israel will not let Palestinians return to their homeland, yet it welcomes Jews from all over the world. It builds houses for its people on land it occupied after the 1967 war, even though the UN has said that the land does not belong to Israel. Israeli planes bomb refugee camps in Arab countries to punish Palestinian guerrillas and innocent people are killed. Yet the guerrillas are fighting for a just cause—an independent Palestinian state that is open to everyone.

We finally ran out of words, or at least out of lengthy declarations. The light faded until we could barely see one another's frowns and smiles. Miriam commented, "It's peaceful here," and after a moment, Ephraim said, "We all need peace."

"A friend of mine belongs to an interfaith committee," Claire said. "She said its aim was to spread understanding and good will. The committee has a feeling that there is good will on both sides. People are tired of the situation as it is. They would like to come to a solution."

"Well," I said, "I'll be going home in a couple of days. When anyone asks me how things are over here, I'll tell them that."

"Good. And then ask them to try to understand us, all of us," Ephraim told me. "We need understanding. We need friends who really know what things are like over here, people who are concerned about peace and justice."

It was time for me to leave; Ephraim had arranged for a limousine to pick me up at 10 o'clock. "We'll make our good-bye here," Claire said. "Miriam knows where the cab stand is."

She took me along a path under the palms, walking slowly. "They would have put you up for the night," she said, "but I asked them not to."

"Why? Are you angry because of what I said on the beach?"

"No. But I can see you tomorrow in Jerusalem and we can talk then. I want to spend some more time with them. And your being here makes me want to think some more about things. Okay?"

"Sure." The limousine waited just ahead, under a street light that glared in bright contrast to the shadowed walk. "May I say good night now?" I asked.

"Yes," she said. And we kissed. Perhaps only to show she wasn't really angry? Oh, no. I could tell.

C H A P T E R
FIVE

SHE called me Friday, as soon as she was in Jerusalem, and told me that she would be staying with the Freijas. "They would like to have you visit us this evening," she said.

"I was hoping to see you alone," I protested. "Can't we get away some place?"

Well, we couldn't, without being discourteous, so I swallowed my disappointment and appeared at the proper time, feeling as if I were making an old-fashioned courting call. Miriam seemed to enjoy the situation; she sat very primly next to me on a sofa but when she said something to me directly I caught hints of teasing laughter in her eyes and in the inflection of her voice. The Freijas were gracious hosts, and our conversation dealt not with war or politics or religion but with Mrs. Freija's interest in Palestinian embroidery and her husband's study of Arabic literature. Finally, when Mr. Freija drove me back to the hotel after both his wife and Miriam had shook my hand in farewell, I had to admit to myself that it had been an unexpectedly happy evening.

When I expressed my appreciation, he waved it aside. "Miriam is a very nice young lady," he told me emphatically. And then he insisted that the next afternoon I borrow his car so that she and I might "see the sights of Palestine," as he put it.

She must have been party to the suggestion, for as soon as I called her the next morning, she suggested an hour. And when she got in the car, she said briskly, "You know, I think I'd like to begin by going to Bethlehem."

"Ma'am," I told her, "for a West Virginia woman, you are mighty bossy with men folk." I started the car and drove two hundred yards, made a turn, and stopped in front of a big canvas-covered watermelon stand. "Before we go any further, I would like to ask you to marry me."

She looked at me and, after a moment, said gently, "I'm not ready to have you say that to me. I'm not sure about what has happened to us. I don't understand it."

"I don't know that I understand either, but I know I love you." I reached out and took her hand. "I think about you all the time, the last thing at night, the first thing in the morning."

Her hand responded to mine, but she said, "You're a lonely man, Amon. You need someone. That's not the same as love. And because you've become my friend—and very dear to me—I'm sorry for your loneliness. Yet being sorry isn't the same thing as being in love."

Before I could answer, a big green melon and a boy's head appeared in the window behind her. Sharp eyes appraised us and the kid grinned. "Nice. Hey, melon, sir? Only one American dollar."

No, no thanks. Cheap, sir, beautiful. No. Two, for one-fifty. No, leave us alone. Sir, picked this morning, beautiful, smell. . . .

I had to drive away, or there would have been melons all over the street.

Miriam was laughing, but enough in control of herself to see the sign at the corner that pointed to Bethlehem. "Turn right!" she said, and we did, at the cost of some of Mr. Freija's tire rubber.

Bethlehem is practically a suburb of Jerusalem, and we used the travel time talking about me. At first, I didn't want to say much about Nancy, but then I realized that I had to, that it was part of me, that Miriam had a right to know if I wanted her to be my wife. We talked, too, about how I'd felt after Nancy's death, how I was just holding on, driving a cab.

"So you see," I said. "There's not much for me to go home to."

By that time, we'd entered the square in Bethlehem's center, and

I was pulling into a parking space.

"How do you feel about that?" she asked me.

I could have said that it made me want to be where she was, but I realized suddenly that those words wouldn't have been right. They would mean that my happiness depended on her; that I, myself, depended on her. Our marriage would depend on her, too. If I really loved her, I could not put that burden on her.

So I shrugged in response, not trusting myself to speak at that moment. We got out of the car and she said, "I think the Church of the Nativity is over there."

There was too much racing inside me. "Can we just walk around for a while?" I asked her. "I don't think I'm in the mood for it right now."

She nodded and we strolled across the lot, up a street lined with gift shops and fruit stores. She slipped her hand in mine and we played tourist for a while—or perhaps, newly-weds.

When we got back to the car, I asked if she would mind if we took a ride in the country. Mrs. Freija had packed a lunch for us; I thought we might find some shady olive tree out in the hills, away from the town's commercialism.

And indeed we did, along a road that swept in long, graceful curves through the rolling, sunlit land. When we put the food aside, I lay back, propped my head on my hand, and looked at her. She smiled at me, tilted her head a little, and inquired, "Yes?"

"I'm just trying to store up what you look like. I am going back tomorrow. You are quite right about me. I shouldn't ask you to marry me."

A shadow touched her eyes and lips and I hurried to say, "Oh, I don't mean that I don't love you. You're right that I need someone. But I know I do love you."

Her eyes held to mine and all the beauty of that lovely land touched the moment.

"I am yet to find myself," she said. "I don't know what God wants me to be. I like you so much, Amon, that I'm frightened at the thought that I may never see you again. But I have to take that chance."

I sat up and our shoulders brushed and we were in each other's arms. After a while, she whispered something in my ear and I murmured, "What?" And she said it again, "The boy with the watermelons. I think he's watching us again."

"Where?" I looked around. Only tawny hills and grey-green trees and bleached blue sky.

She scrambled away, laughing at me. "Oh, I guess it was my imagination."

* * *

Imagination. Sometimes, sitting here at night, writing to her, looking at the photos I took of her that afternoon, I try to use my imagination to take me back again. But it's really no use. I can scratch sparks from my memory but not the heat and light of reality.

And yet I am neither cold nor in the dark. For I find that the Amon Smith who has returned to Clarksburg is not the Amon Smith who went away. Harry Salter helped in that discovery. I went right to his office from the airport. "Well, at least she's all right," he grumbled when I told him what had happened and why she wasn't coming home.

"Oh, she's a lot more than all right," I said.

"Yeah?" His sharp old eyes regarded me. "You look and act like you've been on a vacation at my expense. You're brown. Been swimming a lot?"

No, Harry Salter, not a vacation. Swimming only with my friend Yusuf in Beirut. Wading once with your daughter and Ephraim and his family. Strange you should ask about swimming. I have been along the Nile and dipped into Cairo and felt the ripple of the Spirit in the night outside St. Mark's. I have been touched by currents of faith that live among garbage collectors, refugees, and priests and people who risk their lives in faithfulness to Jesus Christ. I have been immersed in his followers and their neighbors, baptized in the waters of fear, hope, poverty, pain, healing, despair, and love where they live day by day. I have followed a pilgrim through these waters, and become a pilgrim myself.